The Dark Country

by
Dennis Etchison

Alexander Publishing, inc.
Los Angeles

An EMR Book

An EMR Book by Alexander Publishing, inc.
13243 Vanowen Ave. #5
North Hollywood, California   19605

for information write to the above address or email: emr@alexpub.com

First Edition April 1999

ISBN 1-893475-16-6

Acknowledgements:

The stories in this book first appeared in slightly different
form under the following Copyrights:

"IT ONLY COMES OUT AT NIGHT": © 1976 by Kirby McCauley.
"SITTING IN THE CORNER, WHIMPERING QUIETLY": © 1976 by Stuart
    David Schiff
"THE WALKING MAN" © 1976 by Looking Glass Publications, Inc.
"WE HAVE ALL BEEN HERE BEFORE": © 1976 by Stuart David Schiff.
"DAUGHTER OF THE GOLDEN WEST": © 1973 by Dugent Publishing
    Corp. (Originally published as "A Feast For Cathy.")
"THE PITCH": © 1978 by Stuart David Schiff.
"YOU CAN GO NOW": © 1980 by Renown Publications, Inc.
"TODAY'S SPECIAL": © 1972 Dugent Publications, Corp.
"THE MACHINE DEMANDS A SACRIFICE": © 1972 by Dugent Publish-
    ing Corp.
"CALLING ALL MONSTERS": © 1973 by Mercury Press, Inc. Copyright
    assigned to the author.
"THE DEAD LINE": © 1979 by Stuart David Schiff.
"THE LATE SHIFT": © 1980 by Dennis Etchison.
"THE NIGHTHAWK": © 1978 by Charles L. Grant.
"IT WILL BE HERE SOON": © 1979 by Dennis Etchison.
"DEATHTRACKS": © 1981 by Stuart David Schiff.
"THE DARK COUNTRY": © 1981 by Dennis Etchison.

The versions included in this volume — and these versions
alone — represent the definitive texts.

All stories reprinted by permission of the author and the
author's agent, Kirby McCauley.

Dennis Etchison

Table of Contents

Dennis Etchison

INTRODUCTION by Ramsey Campbell

It was about time. I mean the award I presented to Dennis Etchison for "The Dark Country" — the British Fantasy Award for best short story of the year. Though the award should have been presented at the Birmingham fantasy convention, I was forbidden to do so by the committee, which had become estranged from the British Fantasy Society, whose award it was. All this is incidental and not very interesting, except that the way Dennis was denied his moment of glory in front of the audience which was waiting to hear who had won the awards seems frustratingly consistent. Etchison is still far less appreciated than he deserves to be, and it was certainly about time for this book.

And yet for a period in his twenty years of writing he was appearing alongside Stephen King, in alternate issues of Cavalier. What must the readers have made of the oblique and allusive Etchisons which appeared in (continued on page 90) fragments between the nude ladies primly covering their pubes and the body-brief ads, Big Flash, Scuttles and Sling Shot (... a tornado of perfection ... big idea with brief action)? Perhaps they didn't know enough about the conventions to which horror fiction is expected to conform to be deterred by his unpredictability.

I can only think it's that quality which has denied him the fame accorded to so many lesser writers. In these days of super-marketing labels it's dangerous for a writer of HORROR FICTION to break the conventions. Maybe it bothers some readers that some of his tales pursue their themes beyond what would be the conventional punch line, while some do without a punch line entirely. You have my word that he is offering more than bide-bound horror fiction does, not less.

Etchison is a poet of loneliness and alienation, whether in the big city or on the freeway. "You Can Go Now," "The Nighthawk," "It Will Be Here Soon," and "Deathtracks" are four of the most poignant fantasies (which means anything but escapism) of our time. On the other hand, his transplant trilogy is one of the most chilling achievements in contemporary horror I can think of; in particular, "The Dead Line" manages to live up to the most horrifying first line ever written. Etchison has little time as a writer for the manufacturing of atmosphere, and why should he when he can even (in "The Pitch") make a description of food terrifying? Who else in this too often reactionary field has forged so far ahead and kept on while so few people noticed? Now at last the power and range of his work is on display too strikingly to be ignored.

Dennis Etchison is the finest writer of short stories now working in this field, and the rest of us ought to learn from him.

Merseyside, England
22 July 1982

That's what I wrote in 1982. Since then the title story earned the World Fantasy Award as well, thus becoming the first tale to receive the fantasy accolades from both sides of the ocean without containing any fantasy. Sometimes, quite rightly, literary worth is enough. Subsequently Dennis picked up another World Fantasy Award for editing

Metahorror, and two of the British Fantasy variety for "The Olympic Runner" and "The Dog Park". Acclaim remains slower than he deserves, but nevertheless it's the good writers who last, and so here is a welcome revival of his first published collection, which looks more than ever like a classic. I see no reason to change a word of the final line of my original introduction — I'll only exhort the reader to seek out the considerable body of work with which he has graced our field since. So incisive a writer needs courage. May it never desert him.

Wallasey, Merseyside
2 February 1999

Dennis Etchison

IT ONLY COMES OUT AT NIGHT

If you leave L.A. by way of San Bernardino, headed for Route 66 and points east, you must cross the Mojave Desert.

Even after Needles and the border, however, there is no relief; the dry air only thins further as the long, relentless climb continues in earnest. Flagstaff is still almost two hundred miles, and Winslow, Gallup and Albuquerque are too many hours away to think of making without food, rest and, mercifully, sleep.

It is like this: the car runs hot, hotter than it ever has before, the plies of the tires expand and contract until the sidewalls begin to shimmy slightly as they spin on over the miserable Arizona roads, giving up a faint odor like burning hair from between the treads, as the windshield colors over with essence of honeybee, wasp, dragonfly, mayfly, June bug, ladybug and the like, and the radiator, clotted with the bodies of countless kamikaze insects, hisses like a moribund lizard in the sun ...

All of which means, of course, that if you are traveling that way between May and September, you move by night.

Only by night.

For there are, after all, dawn check-in motels, Do Not Disturb signs for bungalow doorknobs; there are diners for mid-afternoon breakfasts, coffee by the carton; there are 24-hour filling stations bright as dreams — Whiting Brothers, Conoco, Terrible Herbst — their flags as unfamiliar as their names, with ice machines, soda machines, candy machines; and there are the sudden, unexpected Rest Areas, just off the highway, with brick bathrooms and showers and electrical outlets, constructed especially for those who are weary, out of money, behind schedule ...

So McClay had had to learn, the hard way.

He slid his hands to the bottom of the steering wheel and peered ahead into the darkness, trying to relax. But the wheel stuck to his fingers like warm candy. Off somewhere to his left, the horizon flickered with pearly luminescence, then faded again to black. This time he did not bother to look. Sometimes, though, he wondered just how far away the lightning was striking; not once during the night had the sound of its thunder reached him here in the car.

In the back seat, his wife moaned.

The trip out had turned all but unbearable for her. Four days it had taken, instead of the expected two-and-a-half; he made a great effort not to think of it, but the memory hung over the car like a thunderhead.

It had been a blur, a fever dream. Once, on the second day, he had been passed by a churning bus, its silver sides blinding him until he noticed a Mexican woman in one of the window seats. She was not looking at him. She was holding a swooning infant to the glass, squeezing water onto its head from a plastic baby bottle to keep it from passing out.

McClay sighed and fingered the buttons on the car radio. He knew he would get nothing from the AM or FM bands, not out here, but he clicked it on anyway. He left the volume and tone controls down, so as not to wake Evvie. Then he punched the seldom-used middle button, the shortwave band, and raised the gain carefully until he could barely hear the radio over the hum of the tires.

Static.

Slowly he swept the tuner across the bandwidth, but there was only white noise. It reminded him a little of the summer rain yesterday, starting back, the way it had sounded bouncing off the windows.

He was about to give up when he caught a voice, crack-ling, drifting in and out. He worked the knob like a safe-cracker, zeroing in on the signal.

A few bars of music. A tone, then the voice again. "... Greenwich Mean Time." Then the station ID.

It was the Voice of America Overseas Broadcast.

He grunted disconsolately and killed it.

His wife stirred.

"Why'd you turn it off?" she murmured. "I was listen-ing to that. Good. Program."

"Take it easy," he said, "easy, you're still asleep. We'll be stopping soon."

"... Only comes out at night," he heard her say, and then she was lost again in the blankets.

He pressed the glove compartment, took out one of the Automobile Club guides. It was already clipped open. McClay flipped on the overhead light and drove with one hand, reading over—for the hundredth time?—the list of motels that lay ahead. He knew the list by heart, but seeing the names again reassured him somehow. Besides, it helped to break the monotony.

It was the kind of place you never expect to find in the middle of a long night, a bright place with buildings (a building, at least) and cars, other cars drawn off the high-way to be together in the protective circle of light.

A Rest Area.

He would have spotted it without the sign. Elevated sodium vapor lighting bathed the scene in an almost peach-colored glow, strikingly different from the cold blue-white sentinels of the Interstate Highway. He had seen other Rest Area signs on the way out, probably even this one. But in daylight the signs had meant nothing more to him than FRONTAGE ROAD or BUSINESS DISTRICT NEXT RIGHT. He wondered if it was the peculiar warmth of light that made the small island of blacktop appear so inviting.

McClay decelerated, downshifted and left Interstate 40.

The car dipped and bumped, and he was aware of the new level of sound from the engine as it geared down for the first time in hours.

He eased in next to a Pontiac Firebird, toed the emergency brake and cut the ignition.

He allowed his eyes to close and his head to sink back into the headrest. At last.

The first thing he noticed was the quiet.

It was deafening. His ears literally began to ring, with the high-pitched whine of a late-night TV test pattern.

The second thing he noticed was a tingling at the tip of his tongue.

It brought to mind a picture of a snake's tongue. Picking up electricity from the air, he thought.

The third was the rustling awake of his wife, in back.

She pulled herself up. "Are we sleeping now? Why are the lights ...?"

He saw the outline of her head in the mirror. "It's just a rest stop, hon. I — the car needs a break." Well, it was true, wasn't it? "You want the rest room? There's one back there, see it?"

"Oh my God."

"What's the matter now?"

"Leg's asleep. Listen, are we or are we not going to get a—"

"There's a motel coming up." He didn't say that they wouldn't hit the one he had marked in the book for another couple of hours; he didn't want to argue. He knew she needed the rest — he needed it too, didn't he? "Think I'll have some more of that coffee, though," he said.

"Isn't any more," she yawned.

The door slammed.

Now he was able to recognize the ringing in his ears for what it was: the sound of his own blood. It almost succeeded in replacing the steady drone of the car.

He twisted around, fishing over the back of the seat for the ice chest.

There should be a couple of Cokes left, at least.

His fingers brushed the basket next to the chest, riffling the edges of maps and tour books, by now reshuffled haphazardly over the first-aid kit he had packed himself (tourniquet, forceps, scissors, ammonia inhalants, Merthiolate, triangular bandage, compress, adhesive bandages, tannic acid) and the fire extinguisher, the extra carton of cigarettes, the remainder of a half-gallon of drinking water, the thermos (which Evvie said was empty, and why would she lie?).

He popped the top of a can.

Through the side window he saw Evvie disappearing around the corner of the building. She was wrapped to the gills in her blanket.

He opened the door and slid out, his back aching.

He stood there blankly, the unnatural light washing over him.

He took a long, sweet pull from the can. Then he started walking.

The Firebird was empty.

And the next car, and the next.

Each car he passed looked like the one before it, which seemed crazy until he realized that it must be the work of the light. It cast an even, eerie tan over the baked metal tops, like orange sunlight through air thick with suspended particles. Even the windshields appeared to be filmed over with a thin layer of settled dust. It made him think of country roads, sundowns.

He walked on.

He heard his footsteps echo with surprising clarity, resounding down the staggered line of parked vehicles. Finally it dawned on him (and now he knew how tired he really was) that the cars must actually have people in them — sleeping people. Of course. Well hell, he thought, watching his step, I wouldn't want to wake anyone. The poor devils.

Besides the sound of his footsteps, there was only the distant *swish* of an occasional, very occasional car on the highway; from here, even that was only a distant hush, growing and then subsiding like waves on a nearby shore.

He reached the end of the line, turned back.

Out of the corner of his eye he saw, or thought he saw, a movement by the building.

The Dark Country   **17**

It would be Evvie, shuffling back.

He heard the car door slam.

He recalled something he had seen in one the tourist towns in New Mexico: circling the park — in Taos, that was where they had been — he had glimpsed an ageless Indian, wrapped in typical blanket, ducking out of sight into the doorway of a gift shop; with the blanket over his head that way, the Indian had somehow resembled an Arab, or so it had seemed to him at the time.

He heard another car door slam.

That was the same day — was it only last week? — that she had noticed the locals driving with their headlights on (in honor of something or other, some regional election, perhaps: "'My face speaks for itself,' drawled Herman J. 'Fashio' Trujillo, Candidate for Sheriff"); she had insisted at first that it must be a funeral procession, though for whom she could not guess.

McClay came to the car, stretched a last time, and crawled back in.

Evvie was bundled safely again in the back seat.

He lit a quick cigarette, expecting to hear her voice any second, complaining, demanding that he roll down the windows, at least, and so forth. But, as it turned out, he was able to sit undisturbed as he smoked it down almost to the filter.

Paguate. Bluewater. Thoreau.

He blinked.

Klagetoh. Joseph City. Ash Fork.

He blinked and tried to focus his eyes from the tail-lights a half-mile ahead to the bug-spattered glass, then back again.

Petrified Forest National Park.

He blinked, refocusing. But it did no good.

A twitch started on the side of his face, close by the corner of his eye.

Rehoboth.

He strained at a road sign, the names and mileages,

but instead a seemingly endless list of past and future shops and detours shimmered before his mind's eye.

I've had it, he thought. Now, suddenly, it was catching up with him, the hours of repressed fatigue; he felt a rushing out of something from his chest. No way to make that motel — hell, I can't even remember the name of it now. Check the book. But it doesn't matter. The eyes. *Can't control my eyes anymore.*

(He had already begun to hallucinate things like tree trunks and cows and Mack trucks speeding toward him on the highway. The cow had been straddling the broken line; in the last few minutes its lowing, deep and regular, had become almost inviting.)

Well, he could try for *any* motel. Whatever turned up next.

But how much farther would that be?

He ground his teeth together, feeling the pulsing at his temples. He struggled to remember the last sign.

The next town. It might be a mile. Five miles. Fifty.

Think! He said it, he thought it, he didn't know which.

If he could just pull over, pull over right now and lie down for a few minutes —

He seemed to see clear ground ahead. No rocks, no ditch. The shoulder, just ahead.

Without thinking he dropped into neutral and coasted, aiming for it.

The car glided to a stop.

God, he thought.

He forced himself to turn, reach into the back seat.

The lid to the chest was already off. He dipped his fingers into the ice and retrieved two half-melted cubes, lifted them into the front seat and began rubbing them over his forehead.

He let his eyes close, seeing dull lights fire as he daubed at the lids, the rest of his face, the forehead again. As he slipped the ice into his mouth and chewed, it broke apart as easily as snow.

He took a deep breath. He opened his eyes again.

At that moment a huge tanker roared past, slamming

an aftershock of air into the side of the car. The car rocked like a boat at sea.

No. It was no good.

So. So he could always turn back, couldn't he? And why not? The Rest Area was only twenty, twenty-five minutes behind him. (Was that all?) He could pull out and hang a U and turn back, just like that. And then sleep. It would be safer there. With luck, Evvie wouldn't even know. An hour's rest, maybe two; that was all he would need.

Unless — was there another Rest Area ahead?

How soon?

He knew that the second wind he felt now wouldn't last, not for more than a few minutes. No, it wasn't worth the chance.

He glanced in the rearview mirror.

Evvie was still down, a lumpen mound of blanket and hair.

Above her body, beyond the rear window, the raised headlights of another monstrous truck, closing ground fast.

He made the decision.

He slid into first and swung out in a wide arc, well ahead of the blast of the truck, and worked up to fourth gear. He was thinking about the warm, friendly lights he had left behind.

He angled in next to the Firebird and cut the lights.

He started to reach for a pillow from the back, but why bother? It would probably wake Evvie, anyway.

He wadded up his jacket, jammed it against the passenger armrest, and lay down.

First he crossed his arms over his chest. Then behind his head. Then he gripped his hands between his knees. Then he was on his back again, his hands at his sides, his feet cramped against the opposite door.

His eyes were wide open.

He lay there, watching chain lightning flash on the horizon.

Finally he let out a breath that sounded like all the

breaths he had ever taken going out at once, and drew himself up.

He got out and walked over to the rest room.

Inside, white tiles and bare lights. His eyes felt raw, peeled. Finished, he washed his hands but not his face; that would only make sleep more difficult.

Outside again and feeling desperately out of synch, he listened to his shoes falling hollowly on the cement.

"Next week we've got to get organized ..."

He said this, he was sure, because he heard his voice coming back to him, though with a peculiar empty resonance. Well, this time tomorrow night he would be home. As unlikely as that seemed now.

He stopped, bent for a drink from the water fountain.

The footsteps did not stop.

Now wait, he thought, I'm pretty far gone, but —

He swallowed, his ears popping.

The footsteps stopped.

Hell, he thought, I've been pushing too hard. We. She. No, it was my fault, my plan this time. To drive nights, sleep days. Just so. As long as you *can* sleep.

Easy, take it easy.

He started walking again, around the corner and back to the lot.

At the corner, he thought he saw something move at the edge of his vision.

He turned quickly to the right, in time for a fleeting glimpse of something — someone — hurrying out of sight into the shadows.

Well, the other side of the building housed the women's rest room. Maybe it was Evvie.

He glanced toward the car, but it was blocked from view.

He walked on.

Now the parking area resembled an oasis lit by firelight. Or a western camp, the cars rimming the lot on three sides in the manner of wagons gathered against the night.

Strength in numbers, he thought.

Again, each car he passed looked at first like every

other. It was the flat light, of course, And of course they were the same cars he had seen a half-hour ago. And the light still gave them a dusty, abandoned look.

He touched a fender.

It *was* dusty.

But why shouldn't it be? His own car had probably taken on quite a layer of grime after so long on these roads.

He touched the next car, the next.

Each was so dirty that he could have carved his name without scratching the paint.

He had an image of himself passing this way again — God forbid — a year from now, say, and finding the same cars parked here. The *same* ones.

What if, he wondered tiredly, what if some of these cars had been abandoned? Overheated, exploded, broken down one fine midday and left here by owners who simply never returned? Who would ever know? Did the Highway Patrol, did anyone bother to check? Would an automobile be preserved here for months, years by the elements, like a snakeskin shed beside the highway?

It was a thought, anyway.

His head was buzzing.

He leaned back and inhaled deeply, as deeply as he could at this altitude.

But he did hear something. A faint tapping. It reminded him of running feet, until he noticed the lamp overhead:

There were hundreds of moths beating against the high fixture, their soft bodies tapping as they struck and circled and returned again and again to the lens; the light made their wings translucent.

He took another deep breath and went on to his car.

He could hear it ticking, cooling down, before he got there. Idly he rested a hand on the hood. Warm, of course. The tires? He touched the left front. It was taut, hot as a loaf from the oven. When he took his hand away, the color of the rubber came off on his palm like burned skin.

He reached for the door handle.

A moth fluttered down onto the fender. He flicked it

off, his finger leaving a streak on the enamel.

He looked closer and saw a wavy, mottled pattern covering his unwashed car, and then he remembered. The rain, yesterday afternoon. The rain had left blotches in the dust, marking the finish as if with dirty fingerprints.

He glanced over at the next car.

It, too, had the imprint of dried raindrops — but, close up, he saw that the marks were superimposed in layers, over and over again.

The Firebird had been through a great many rains.

He touched the hood.

Cold.

He removed his hand, and a dead moth clung to his thumb. He tried to brush it off on the hood, but other moth bodies stuck in its place. Then he saw countless shriveled, mummified moths pasted over the hood and top like peeling chips of paint. His fingers were coated with the powder from their wings.

He looked up.

High above, backed by banks of roiling cumulous clouds, the swarm of moths vibrated about the bright, protective light.

So the Firebird had been here a very long time.

He wanted to forget it, to let it go. He wanted to get back in the car, He wanted to lie down, lock it out, everything. He wanted to go to sleep and wake up in Los Angeles.

He couldn't.

He inched around the Firebird until he was facing the line of cars. He hesitated a beat, then started moving.

A LeSabre.

A Cougar.

A Chevy van.

A Corvair.

A Ford.

A Mustang.

And every one was overlaid with grit.

He paused by the Mustang. Once — how long ago? — it had been a luminous candy-apple red; probably belonged to a teenager. Now the windshield was opaque, the body dulled to a peculiar shade he could not quite place.

Feeling like a voyeur at a drive-in movie theater, McClay crept to the driver's window.

Dimly he perceived two large outlines in the front seat.

He raised his hand.

Wait.

What if there were two people sitting there on the other side of the window, watching him?

He put it out of his mind. Using three fingers, he cut a swath through the scum on the glass and pressed close.

The shapes were there. Two headrests.

He started to pull away.

And happened to glance into the back seat.

He saw a long, uneven form.

A leg, the back of a thigh. Blond hair, streaked with shadows. The collar of a coat.

And, delicate and silvery, a spider web, spun between the hair and collar.

He jumped back.

His leg struck the old Ford. He spun around, his arms straight. The blood was pounding in his ears.

He rubbed out a spot on the window of the Ford and scanned the inside.

The figure of a man, slumped on the front seat.

The man's head lay on a jacket. No, it was not a jacket. It was a large, formless stain. In the filtered light, McClay could see that it had dried to a dark brown.

It came from the man's mouth.

No, not from the mouth.

The throat had a long, thin slash across it, reaching nearly to the ear.

He stood there stiffly, his back almost arched, his eyes jerking, trying to close, trying not to close. The lot, the even light reflecting thinly from each windshield, the Corvair, the van, the Cougar, the LeSabre, the suggestion of a shape within each one.

The pulse in his ears muffled and finally blotted out the

distant gearing of a truck up on the highway, the death-rattle of the moths against the seductive lights.

He reeled.

He seemed to be hearing again the breaking open of doors and the scurrying of padded feet across paved spaces.

He remembered the first time. He remembered the sound of a second door slamming in a place where no new car but his own had arrived.

Or — had it been the door to his car slamming a second time, after Evvie had gotten back in?

If so, how? Why?

And there had been the sight of someone moving, trying to slip away.

And for some reason now he remembered the Indian in the tourist town, slipping out of sight in the doorway of that gift shop. He held his eyelids down until he saw the shop again, the window full of kachinas and tin gods and tapestries woven in a secret language.

At last he remembered it clearly: the Indian had not been entering the store. *He bad been stealing away*

McClay did not understand what it meant, but he opened his eyes, as if for the first time in centuries, and began to run toward his car.

If I could only catch my goddamn breath, he thought.

He tried to hold on. He tried not to think of her, of what might have happened the first time, of what he may have been carrying in the back seat ever since.

He had to find out.

He fought his way back to the car, against a rising tide of fear he could not stem.

He told himself to think of other things, of things he knew he could control: mileages and motel bills, time zones and weather reports, spare tires and flares and tubeless repair tools, hydraulic jack and Windex and paper towels and tire iron and socket wrench and waffle cushion and travelers checks and credit cards and Dopp Kit (toothbrush and paste, deodorant, shaver, safety blade, brushless cream) and sunglasses and Sight Savers and teargas pen

The Dark Country   **25**

and fiber-tip pens and portable radio and alkaline batteries and fire extinguisher and desert water bag and tire guage and motor oil and his moneybelt with identification sealed in plastic —

In the back of his car, under the quilt, nothing moved, not even when he finally lost his control and his mind in a thick, warm scream.

SITTING IN THE CORNER, WHIMPERING QUIETLY

It was one of those bright places you never expect to find in the middle of the night, a place of porcelain and neon lighting and whitewashed walls. I walked in with my old army bag stuffed full of a month's dirty clothes and swung it on top of one of the long line of waiting, open washing machines.

A quarter to three in the morning.

And nobody in sight for miles and miles.

I let out a sigh, which not surprisingly turned into a yawn, and felt for the change in my pocket.

I didn't see her at first. That is to say, I knew she was there without turning around. I think it was the cigarette smoke. It cut a sharp edge through the hot, stifling, humid dryer air that hung so thick in the laundromat you felt you could stick out your finger and jab a hole in it.

"Well, he finally got what he wanted."

I moved along the wall to the corner detergent dispenser. It was very late and I couldn't sleep and I had come here to be alone, just to have something to do and to be left alone to do it, and I was in no mood to try my hand at winning friends and influencing people.

I heard water running in the sink next to me.

"That's what he thought, all right." Her voice came very close to me now, going on as if picking up a running conversation we might have been having.

I turned my head just long enough for a quick glance at her.

She was young but not too, twenty-nine going on forty, and pretty, too, but not really very. She had long hair hanging down to the middle of her thin back, with blond streaks bleached in, *très chic,* you know, and one of her phony eyelashes was coming unglued in the warm, wet air.

"A house in the Valley, two cars — no, three — paid vacation in the Virgin Islands, and a son, yeah, a little Vladimir Jr. to carry on his glorious family name. Just like he always wanted. But that was *all* he wanted — that's the part they never tell you in front."

She dropped the butt of her Pall Mall and lit another at once, pulling long, hard drags down into her lungs.

"Last week the kid took the gun from the closet and walked up to me in the kitchen," she continued, starting to hand-wash a sheet in the sink. "Pointed it right at my head and said, 'Bang, you're dead, Mommy.' 'Well,' I said, 'are you gonna do it or not? Don't ever point one of those things at someone unless you're gonna use it.'

"So he did. The kid pulled the trigger. I didn't think he had the guts. 'Course it wasn't loaded. That *really* pissed me off. It was just like Vladimir, not teaching him what it means to be a — but what would his dad know about that? About what it takes to be a man."

She scrubbed at the soiled sheet, pausing to jerk a wet hand up to move a strand of hair away from her face. I couldn't help taking a better look at her face then. It was like the rest of her, young and yet old, drawn and tight, made up expensively even now, in the middle of the night, though obviously in haste, and tired, and blank. For a second then, overpoweringly, I had the belief that she was the same young/old woman I had seen seated in the window of a beauty salon in Beverly Hills once; and later, in a cocktail lounge with another girl, waiting, with long, sharp fingernails the color of blood. French-inhaling a Marlboro and with a look on her face that told you she had a hundred dollar bill in her purse. And that she was waiting. Just waiting.

She picked up her Pall Mall with a wet thumb and first finger, drawing hard.

I noticed the clock on the wall: three o'clock.

"That was when I got it. All these years, trying to figure a way to teach him and that God damned kid of his something."

I fed a couple of nickles into the detergent machine.

She paused long enough to take a couple of more lengthy hits from her Pall Mall. It was so quiet you could hear the sound of the smoke blowing out into the white light.

"So tonight he comes home and makes the pitcher of martinis, as usual, and goes into his room and closes the door. I go to the door and ask him what the hell's wrong *this* time. He says he doesn't know. He just wants me to leave him alone."

She laughed startlingly, hoarsely.

"Okay, hot shot, I'll leave you the hell alone, I think. You wanna come home from your fucking office looking like a corpse again tonight and lay around until you fall asleep for the zillionth time? All right, I'll let you!"

"We'll find out if that's what you really want."

"Only first you and that little pussy of a son of yours are gonna get a lesson you'll never forget."

She turned on the water full force. It gushed out, flooding the basin faster than it could empty.

"Who ever said if you wash it in cold water it'll come out. *Damn.* Why the hell did I have to give him the striped sheets, anyway?

"So I wake the kid up. It doesn't matter — he's awake, and the bed's all wet as usual. I ask him if he remembers what I taught him."

"It takes a minute or two, but he finally catches on, the dumb little bastard."

"So I go get the bullets down and tell him to go in there and prove to me that he remembers what it was I beat the shit out of him for last week ..."

I started to dump my stuff into a machine at the far end of the room. Then, all of a sudden, the thread of what she had been saying got through to me.

I turned back to look at her.

She was grinding a bar of soap into the sheet now. At the edges the spot was a thick brown, almost black, but at the heart I noticed it was still a deep, gummy shade close to the color of her nails as her fingers flashed violently around the material. The steam was rising up from the basin to surround her.

I closed my eyes fast.

Outside, a car came suddenly from nowhere and passed hurriedly by, swishing away down the empty boulevard.

She finished the story. I didn't want to hear it, tried to block it out of my ears but she told it through to the finish. It didn't matter to her. She had never been talking to me anyway.

My eyes jammed shut, harder and harder, until I saw gray shapes that seemed to move in front of me. Never before in my life up to that moment could I remember feeling so detached, so out of it. I leaned the heels of my hands against the washer. The quarter slipped from my fingers, clanked against the enamel and hit the cold, cracked cement floor.

The last thing I heard her saying was:

"... So afterward I tell the kid to go back to bed, to go to sleep, just to go the hell to sleep, but he can't. Or won't. He just sits there on the floor in the corner, the gun still in his lap, whimpering quietly. That was how I left him, the little sissy ..."

Disgusted — tired and sick and disgusted out of all memory and beyond all hope — I forced my things back into the bag and stumbled out of the laundromat. She said something after me but I didn't want to hear what it was.

I pulled my coat up around my ears. I was starting to shiver. I snorted, at no one in particular, at the night and all the people in it, everywhere, the stupid, unthinking people who don't know enough to leave a man alone, just to leave you the hell alone the times when you need it most. There was no place left for me to go, no place at all anywhere in the city. And so, breathing steam, I made it away from there as fast as I could, heading off down the street in the same direction as the car and blinking fast, being careful not to step on any cracks, all the way back to my room. My quiet room.

Dennis Etchison

THE WALKING MAN

It was one of those long, blue evenings that come to the Malibu late in the year, the water undulating up to the beach like some smooth, sleepy girl moving slowly under a satin sheet. I must have been staring, because the bartender leaned over and pushed the empty glass against the back of my hand.

"Another?"

"Vodka," I reminded him. The sky, out by the point that shelters the Colony, was turning a soft, tropical orange of the kind one expects to see only on foreign postage stamps. The edge of the water lapped the pilings below the restaurant. An easy, regular rhythm, like the footsteps outside on the pier.

He reached for a dry napkin. "Live around here?"

"A few months," I told him. It was still true, for the moment, at least. I hoped he would let it pass. I didn't want to go into the alimony and the rest of it, not now.

He had the Rose's Lime Juice in his hand. The way he handled it, I could see he hadn't been at this too long. He was young, still in his twenties; I wondered how he had got the job with all that sun-bleached hair. "Should've seen it back about May, June," he said. He picked up a cherry, one of the green ones, but I held up my hand and he put it back. "All that sand out there?"

I turned back to the window and looked with him.

"Rocks," he said. I heard the rough ice cubes drop into the glass.

"Right."

"Out there, I mean. Boulders like you never seen. Like the moon or something. Five, six feet of sand must've washed in over the summer."

He was right. I remembered the beach below the sun deck of our newly leased house: the sand slick as a wet peach as far as we could walk at low tide, and piled in solid around the posts; and I remembered waking one morning to find it gone, washed out from under us during the night, everything but the rocky underpinnings, all the way out to the tide pools where mussels held to the sharp erosions, crusted hard against the beaks of the circling gulls. Now, the season and the waterline changing, it was all coming back. I remembered, and he was right.

The drink was up. I started on it. The kitchen wouldn't be serving for another hour and the room was still empty, even here at the bar. There were a couple of too-young waitresses making like they were busy, wiping off the plastic menus and refilling the little bowls with sugar packets. I sat watching them in the light of the sunset, their figures silhouetted against the empty panes, but I knew all about the game and I didn't feel up to it. They looked like nervous laughs and weekends at Mammoth and a taste for cold duck, and when they joked at each other under their breaths the sound came to me above the piped-in music: telephone voices just out of the shower, brittle as window glass, unexpectedly cold, and transparent.

There wasn't much left of the drink so I turned on the stool for one last view. I knew I couldn't see my place from here, buried past a stretch of big rich ones, but I tried just the same.

"Which one?"

The voice was so flat, so toneless the thought occurred that it might have been my own. I drained the glass against my teeth and put it down. The bartender was twisting some bottles of Bud in shaved ice. He flicked his eyes in what I took to be the direction of the color TV, but it wasn't on. It never was. I leaned in, trying to see past the end of the bar.

She was back there at the small table, the one you never notice against the wood. I wouldn't have spotted her at all except for her eyes, the way the whites reflected the dim light coming through the stained glass porthole on the side door. They were huge, very wide-set, as if drawn by a Forties comic strip artist; I couldn't place the style. They were not looking at me. I squinted anyway, trying to see into the shadows. But she was not looking at me.

Something small and white lifted to her lips. No, I thought, or maybe I muttered it. Not this time, and I did not reach for the matches on the bar.

Then she did something I wasn't ready for, something that had a little class, just a little, at least. She went ahead and lit the cigarette, without the look, the wait. And suddenly I felt bitter in the throat at myself as well as the game, at the whole thing, just the whole damn thing.

"The lady," said the bartender. "I think she's talking to you."

She still wasn't looking at me. "What did she say?"

"Don't ask me, man," he said, and he winked. That settled it for me. No way.

"No way," I said.

He shrugged. I climbed off the stool. He was watching but I wasn't going to give him the next act. "Set up one more," I told him. "I'm going to the head."

"Sure," he said. You know how he said it.

I took a couple of steps. Then I remembered about the head. (A varnished plaque on the door: BUCKS.) It was back there, down a hail between the cigarette machine and the pay phone. The hall next to the small table.

Well, the hell with her.

I passed the table. I was about to turn into the hall, but I couldn't resist checking her out, just once. Call it a flaw in my character, an itch in the place you know you can't scratch but can't stop yourself from trying, every time.

There was something I recognized. Maybe she

reminded me of the types in the class Beverly Hills saloons with the Boston ferns hanging from the ceiling, the ones I've seen as I passed by outside the glass: twenty-nine going on forty, skin diet-taut, a streak bleached into the hair; a look that says that she's got a C-note folded in her bag and that she's waiting, just waiting. This one had the expression, I guess, but that was all. Her hair was black, no streak. Not shiny black, but dull, more like what's left in the grate a minute before the fire goes out. Drawn back along the sides of her head, but not tight, not a cheap face-lift, not like she cared. Her skin was white, but not kept from the sun like some courtesan; it was the kind of pale you get when you don't care enough to go outside.

And there were the eyes. They set me on edge. They were too extreme, like something you learn never to expect in this life: gilt on the lily, egg in the beer, too much, much too much for the way they tell you things are supposed to be.

"Which one," she said, again. She said it that way, not a question, not anything.

"Don't worry. You couldn't see my house if you tried." *Don't worry. You couldn't see my house if you tried.* I said it, I thought it, I don't know which.

"Will you help me?"

She did not bother to raise her head.

"Which one? Which one of those people?" she continued.

Now I knew we weren't on the same wavelength. I had no idea what she was talking about.

Her eyes were fixed somewhere close to the line of houses. The pier, I gathered. A few tourists were out on the boards, strolling up and back, back and up. They reminded me of shooting gallery targets, rolling along on tracks and wobbling a little in the breeze. Except that I could hear footsteps, even here.

"What about them?" I asked.

"They remind me of mannequins." She stubbed out

her cigarette, almost new. "Do mannequins have wheels, do you know?"

I was standing there looking down at her, studying her face. It was an exaggerated triangle, inverted — like the Sub-Mariner, I think, if you remember. Then again, maybe it was only the perspective. "That's a funny thing to say," I said.

"Which one would you kill," she said. Another non-question. "Say you could name your price. Any one you choose."

I thought about it, I don't know why. She was making some kind of point, I guess. I wanted to hear what it was. "You talk like they're not even human," I said.

She raised her face a few degrees. Her chin was really tiny, almost lost below her enormous lower lip, which was puffed out in a perpetual pout. More than anything else, I saw her wide, pallid forehead. She had not arranged her hair to hide it.

"And we are?" she said. "Is that what you mean?"

I leaned on the rail and watched the water bringing sand up to the shoreline. Bringing it up or taking it away.

"Say you had to choose."

I pivoted, startled but not surprised. She had come up like a ghost, one of those with sheet trailing and no feet below to sound the boards. I turned back to the rail. The gulls were swooping on the pearled waters, trying to pick up fish that had come too close to shore, into the tide pools between the green rocks where they didn't belong.

I heard her release a long, shuddering breath. With effort, her voice low, she said, "If you won't say it, I'll say it for you. You can't choose because it wouldn't make any difference. You can't tell them apart."

I shut my eyes and held them shut for a while before I opened them. Shadows on the sand. People on the beach. Figures chasing a ball, picking driftwood, unleashing dogs, rolling trouser legs, walking hand in hand. I couldn't see their faces from here. Each time my eyes opened the configuration was different, the figures shuffled, interchanged.

But I was letting myself go. It was easy. Too easy.

I pressed my eyelids shut again, so tight I saw dull light.

Thinking: well all right, why not, maybe this one is different, I pulled myself up. Finding the strength, blinking, I faced her with eyes open. I reached down, steeling myself and relaxing, setting and going with it. Hands on the rail behind, the nails whitened moons, they must have been, I heard myself saying, "What is it you really want?"

I left the lights off.

She wanted me, but not desperately. She gave, but not to lose herself. She took from me — received and did not grasp. The moment did seem to be out of time, but passed to the next moment as easily as the passing of a breath. I began to think of her as beautiful. She might have been anyone. She was familiar somehow; I had never known her like. I passed from her back into myself as easily as a breath is taken and released. I was aware of the wind outside, the lights in the windows of other houses going on and off along the point, the white sound of the waves, the passing and repassing of slapping feet on the beach, drunken laughter beyond the deck. The absence of laughter. The easy silence, and the night.

"Who's out there?"

"What? Nobody, probably. It's late."

"I don't mean the beach. I thought I heard someone walking. Outside, there."

She meant the front of the house. "There's nothing out there but the highway. Not even a sidewalk, You know that."

I watched her in the moonlight from the window.

"All right, what is it?"

She shifted to her side, her hair lifting away from the pillow in long black tendrils. "Sometimes there's a man, walking."

I reached for my shirt. "Smoke?"

"Mm."

But before I could get to my cigarettes, she had one in her mouth. I don't know where she got it. I gave her a light. I saw the twisted end, the way it caught and burned unevenly.

She filled her lungs without blinking and held out the joint.

I hesitated, but only for a second. The last couple of times it had made me remember too much, had made the ache come again. I took it. It tasted like sweet garbage, but it went down easy.

She lay back. Her eyes were staring. I seemed to be seeing her from above: the dark hollows over her collarbone, her breasts, the way they did not flatten when she lay on her back, the way her breath moved below her ribs, the tangle between her thighs, glistening under me ...

"How do you know no one is there?" she said.

"Because —" I flopped onto my back, took another lungful, executed a quick sit-up. I crossed the living room, drew open the top half of the door to the sun deck and leaned out. The tide was low, a good fifty feet from the supports, and nothing was moving but a line of sandpipers between the naked rocks. "Becausethere's nobody. On the beach or anywhere else around here." With irritation. "What's the —" *matter with you,* I started to say.

"How do you know?" she repeated.

My mouth opened. It stayed open, my jaw scissoring as I came back to the big pillows. I squatted next to her on the rug, almost over her. "I need some more of that, I guess," I said, reaching for the joint, "before I can pick up what you're trying to say."

She punched up the pillow.

"We were talking about something, back on the pier," she said. "Remember?"

Though she would not meet my eyes, I stared at her. I thought her mouth began to move, but it was only her chin, receding further.

Get it out, I thought. The rest of it, so that I can know what to think of you, before I let myself think any more of you than I do. "Come on." Or do you want to go back into hiding in that bar, I thought, do you really? Is that all you want? "Damn it," I said, "you're —" spooking me, I thought. *Really.*

"I'm what?" She rose up on the pillow.

"Nothing."

"That's what I thought," she said, slumping.

"Oh God."

"All right," she said. "Only first you have to tell me something."

Let this be good, I thought, and let it be quick.

"Just this," she said. "When was the first time you heard the voice?"

I didn't say anything.

"For me," she said, her tone unchanged, "it was only after I started having the dreams. They got so bad that for a while I was afraid to go to sleep. But then, the first time I heard it, I was finally able to give up the ghost. Just like that. I woke up laughing, and I knew the world was mine."

I got up. I sat down. Then I got up again and went around the bookcase to the kitchen. The water felt good on my face. I tried to make it last.

"Well?" she asked. "Will you do it?"

I lit a cigarette. It was getting cold. I wanted to close a window, but none was open.

"You know you've thought about it. Admit it. It could happen anywhere. In the middle of the night, in a place you've never been before, a place where no one knows you. Glendale, Upland, Paso Robles, it doesn't matter. Anywhere at all."

Her voice rose half an octave, like a violin string tightening, winding up. She took a deep breath.

"You're driving down an empty street at three o'clock in the morning, say. All the TV sets are off. The police cars are parked at the House of Pies. You don't know where you're going. You turn corners. Then you see someone, sooner or later you always do. He could be anyone. He's walking alone, hurrying home under the trees, the leaves are cracking under his feet like bones. You cut the lights and as you pass you feel the gun in your hand and your finger on the trigger and — and it doesn't matter.

"Or maybe you wait until he crosses the street. You dare yourself not to hit the brakes, and — and all there is is a sound. And he's gone. He never was. And it doesn't matter."

Her voice was rhythmic, incantatory.

I let her go on.

"Or in an all-night laundromat, And the knife is there in your pocket, the way you knew it would be when you needed it. Or you feel your hands on a throat in the back row of a movie theater. Or standing on a cliff over the rocks. And your hands want to push. Or under a pier with only the waves, and you see him, and suddenly you feel the rock in your hand. And it doesn't matter. Somewhere, anywhere, even right here, why not? It doesn't matter, In the middle of the night with no one to see ..."

I locked my knees. I dug my heels into the jute carpeting and set my back against the wall.

"So why don't you?" I couldn't think of anything else to say.

"Why don't you?" she said quickly.

The cigarette tip made a track in the air. I watched it.

"Because you've never understood the feeling," she continued, "until now. It's never been verified. You might be crazy. It's easy to think that. One alone is weak. But two is a point of view."

Her words began to lose all meaning. They might have been sounds made by a pointed stick on a fence at midnight.

"So name your price," she said.

"Why?"

"Oh, the money will make it easier the first time. It gives you a reason you can live with. That's only practical."

Practical.

"Five thousand," she said.

"Why?"

"Ten. Oh, I have it, don't worry."

"But why me?"

"Your eyes," she said. "The way you kept looking around every time somebody walked by on the pier. As if you almost expected to see yourself."

I just looked at her. I don't know if she could see me.

"Twenty-five thousand dollars," she said. "I can get it. Everyone has his price. *Doesn't he.*"

I tried to walk. The room moved before me. I saw her as if from a great distance, from the ceiling? The top of the head, the part in the hair like a white scar, the high cheekbones, the bony shoulders, the hands holding the knees, the knees like second breasts, the knuckles like worn-down teeth. I moved past her. Outside, a full moon hung over the water.

"Listen," I heard her say, "you won't even have to choose. That's the hard part, isn't it? Well, I've already found one for you. There's one I always see, a man with his dog, back there between the rocks. You'll know him — the dog's crippled. Always the same time, every night. And he's old. It will be so easy. No one will see. Use anything you want."

For a time, I don't know how long, I balanced there. The white sound was blowing in from the ocean.

"You see?" she was saying. "I need someone. I need to know, to be free and know that I'm free. You will be free, too. We will be the fortunate ones, because we'll know no remorse."

I faced her.

"The voice," she said, "remember the voice."

She reached to touch me.

"Everybody has a price," she said.

I had not realized until that moment how unfeeling she was. Her touch was almost cruel; her words were almost kind.

"That may be true enough," I said slowly.

"How much is it worth, then?"

"Nothing."

Then I just waited.

"And we are?" she said.

I took a long time trying to think of a way to answer her.

Now the circling gulls were gone; only a single king-fisher remained to patrol the waters.

I walked, touching each post on the pier.

At first the sound was so familiar I didn't notice it.

The sound of footsteps.

Without looking up, I stopped by the rail.

The footsteps stopped.

Below the pier, the skin of the sand had been polished to an unearthly sheen. I stood there, looking down.

"You got a light, by any chance?" said a voice.

It was a man I had seen walking the boards earlier.

I told him I didn't.

"Don't ever depend on these throwaway lighters," he said, clicking the wheel uselessly against the flint. "Once they're empty, they're not worth a dime."

He pitched it underhand into the water. It fell end-over-end, disappearing from sight.

"The bar has matches," I said.

He made no move to leave. Instead he leaned his back against the rail.

I shifted and glanced around.

Back at the bar, on the other side of the glass, bodies were moving, rearranging. I couldn't help but notice. The filtered moonlight caught one face out of all the others, at the small table by the hall to the cigarette machine and the pay phone.

I must have stared for a long time. Then I got it, finally.
Kirby.

I said it, I thought it, I don't know which.

"Who?"

"Kirby," I said, snapping my fingers again. He was old enough to remember, so I went on. "A comic book artist, back in the Forties. See that girl in there, the one with the face like a broken moon? She looks like she was drawn by

Jack Kirby." A portrait of Poe's sister, in fact, but I didn't say that.

There was no reason he should have answered. He probably thought I was crazy.

I turned oceanward again.

The moonlight had broken up on the surface of the water now, like so much shattered mercury. I watched the edges of the tide foaming around the pilings, bringing a wet, white reflection to the hidden rocks.

His elbow was almost touching mine. He was already off-balance. It wouldn't have taken much to send him backwards over the edge.

I said to the man, "How would you like to set someone free for me." It was somewhere between a statement and a question. "Lean on, snuff. For money, of course. It'll have to be on the installment plan. But for her, I'll come up with a hell of a down payment."

I felt a laugh starting, deep down.

"Come on, come on," I said, "what's your price, man? Everybody has his price, doesn't he?"

"Yeah," he said right off. He had been following it. "Only sometimes," he said, playing it out, "it may not be worth paying."

I managed a look at him. His face was leathery, but the skin around the eyes was still soft. He squinted, and a hundred tiny crinkles appeared.

"Before you say any more," he said, "I ought to let you in on something. I guess I ought to tell you that I'm what they call a private investigator."

I couldn't read his expression.

"I also ought to give you a free piece of advice," he said. "You seem like a decent guy. Do yourself a favor. Drop it right now."

"What?" I tried to get a fix on him. "Is she a client of yours or something?"

"The husband, pal," he said confidentially.

"I think you're trying to tell me something. So who is he?"

He gazed off down the beach. He gave a nod, meaning, I figured, one of the big stilt houses, the ones with the floodlights aimed at the waves.

Then I noticed something moving.

It looked like a man. I watched as the figure passed between the pilings, laying a long, stooped, crooked shadow over the stones.

"He looks old," I said.

"And rich," said the detective, if that's what he was. "Filthy, like Midas. Otherwise I wouldn't be bothered. Domestic surveillance isn't my style. Can't take the hours anymore."

"Wait a minute," I said. "The old man. The husband." It stuck in my throat. "He has a dog, right? And he takes it for walks. Same time, every night?"

"Take a look. Christ, the mutt's only got three fucking legs. Can you beat that?"

I couldn't.

"He's got an idea she's a tramp, you get the drift? So I tail her. Everywhere. I should blush to tell you how much he pays me. But all I got to do is wait and watch."

"No, I can't beat that, man," I said. "I really can't."

And started walking.

And heard footsteps on the pier, *footsteps echoed as from far below,* my footsteps, saw shoes falling on the boards, *my shoes when I looked for them seemed very far away* my shoes, *as I watched the water, then the sand under the pier,* the cracks between the planks shuttering over the sand, *and I saw as from a height, the distance growing, from all angles, directions, lengths, myself there,* the sand pocked with breathing holes leading to sand crabs, remains of mussels, clams, oysters, lobster, squid, anemones, puffers, eel, sea snakes, sharks, rays, barracuda, lungfish, trilobites, sea spiders, spiny horrors, sentinels buried in the layered scape, *as I approached the bar,* footsteps passing the split moorings, *the black layers on the roof,* drying ropes frayed by the sojourns of rats from out the tumbling foundations, *the high tilted windows, their panes pulsing with the passing of the tide, the frames beginning to crack,* footsteps, *giving in, giving out,* my footsteps *the laughter and the absence of laughter* nearing the wooden buildings, the restaurant, the bar *beating like wings against the glass.*

And I watched her.

WE HAVE ALL BEEN HERE BEFORE

She sat in the concrete building, in an office with frosted glass partitions and barred windows, her fingers moving like praying mantises on the table. Her eyes half-closed, she saw:

A body. The body of a woman. The nude body of a young woman, the shiny flesh slipping from its bones, floating face up in a swimming pool. What was left of the face.

"Right," someone said, after she told them.

Her eyes were still rolled up. She squirmed in her straight-backed chair, struggling against the rattle of type-writers from the next room, and said, "And there is another one."

"That's news," said the Chief. To one of his men, a lieutenant, he said, "Better check it out. Ask Fitz to run the list again, will you, Billy? You never know." Then, "Where? Can you tell us that?"

"I see ... trees. A hill. A river. Stream. It was a stream, but now it's a river. The rains, yes. The rains. The rains did it."

He leaned over her to see that the tape recorder was still on. "Isn't there something else, Polly?" he asked gently. "Take your time, now."

"No." She began swaying. "Yes. A tower. Airport nearby. Yes. Control tower ..."

The Chief nodded, smiling. "Now tell us about the

man, Polly. Tell me about the man who did it."

"The man?" she said faintly. "Oh yes, the man. I see ... red Pendleton shirt. Trousers filthy. Mud. Driving away. Old car, can't see ...

"Wait. Yes. Apartment. Two oak trees. Dead-end street. West side of town. Pink stucco building."

She fell silent, breathing heavily, her eyeballs straining behind the lids.

The lieutenant hadn't moved. He stood at the door, his hand frozen on the knob. The Chief jerked a thumb at him impatiently, motioning him out.

"Blood," she said abruptly. "Face. Skin." She scraped at her arms. "Washing the blood off. It won't ..."

The Chief put a hand out to steady her.

She stiffened, arching her back. "Branford Way," she said matter-of-factly. "Seventeen-something. Sixth door, on top. A black Toyota in the garage. No, on the street. Always park on the street. Kids play in the garage. The sixth apartment. Six. Six ..."

The Chief looked at the other men. He winked.

"She's got it," he said. "Just like she got the Valley Strangler and — what did the papers call the other one? That creep at the University, remember?"

"The Library Rapist," said one of the men, snickering.

"Right," said the Chief.

He moved with them to a corner of the room.

"Now go out and get on the horn — I want every available unit over there so fast he won't know what hit him. And get this. No leaks this time, understand? Tell the Information Officer that this investigation is strictly SOP. That's the official line, got it? We're pursuing leads, searching the area, blah blah. He can give the press the bit about the latent print if he wants. C.I.D. says it can't be traced, of course, it's not clear enough, but don't tell Riley that. I don't trust that son of a bitch."

"What do you want on the warrant?"

"Shove the warrant! Go in on narco, traffic tickets, any damn thing, I don't care, but get in."

Suddenly the woman slumped forward and rested her

head on her wrists.

"Wait," said the Chief.

He hovered over her again, his tie flopping against the worn surface of the table.

"Polly? Can you hear me?"

She inhaled deeply. Then she sat up, blinking rapidiy, as if awakening from a dream.

"Hi, Jack," she said. "How'd I do?"

"Like a top. You did it again, babe. How do you feel?"

"Oh, I'm fine," she said. "Swell." She rubbed her eyes. "Hey, what're those two guys doing hiding in the corner?" She made a raspy laugh. "What'd I do, say something about their sex lives?"

"What sex lives?" said the Chief. "You were right on the money, babe. You hit it. Didn't she hit it? Everything. The hill, the pool, the victim, And the creep. You're batting a thousand today, doll."

"Don't I always? Hey, look at them. I must've popped their virgin ears. Who's got a smoke?"

The men patted themselves down. The Chief tossed a pack of Viceroys on the table. Then he took a disposable lighter out of his coat pocket and waited while she smoothed her hair and dug out one of the cigarettes with her fingernails. A tremor passed through her hands.

"Oh, I can still see it," she said, shuddering. "The trees and the mud. The pool. And the body. How do you suppose it stayed in the pool for so long, Jack, without anybody noticing?"

"You said it yourself, Poll, remember?" He reached for a file folder, removed a newspaper clipping which he handed to her. "It was the rain. The rain did it."

She read the headline.

47 *Bodies Reburied*
ORPHANS OF THE STORM

"Oh, I remember that," she said, scanning the article. "It was on the wire services, even back where I live." She asked. "What a horrible, horrible story."

"It happened over by the Point," said the Chief. "The February rains were just too much, apparently. After that last storm, forty-some bodies came floating up out of their graves — that's the estimate. Some slid down the hill next to the cemetery, into the road, into back yards, even into swimming pools like this one did. They came right up out of the mud that way, like earthworms, I reckon. Right out of their coffins and down the hill. They still haven't found 'em all. Grisly story, all right," he added with a chuckle.

She made another sound with her tongue. "I still don't get it," she said. "How did your people know that the one in the pool hadn't just, you know, been buried up there like the rest?"

"She had, she had," said the Chief. "But not as a certified interment, you see. Someone — our man in the red shirt now, thanks to you — murdered her, hid her along with the gun in one of the fresh graves sometime around Christmas. We were there when the Forest Glade people came in with their bulldozers for the mass reburial. The city ended up footing the bill for something like fifteen grand in mudslide damages, by the way. And while they were busy tagging the remains, they found a bullet hole in this one's skull. Polly, there's one more detail I—"

The Chief turned, remembering his men.

"So what are you two gawking at? Haven't you ever seen a real live psychic before?"

As he snapped orders and sent them out, she dipped further into the news story. She didn't really want to read it, but she was both repelled and fascinated by the details.

She hadn't known what she would be in for when she accepted the invitation to fly out this morning. She had worked with police departments all over the country in these last eight years, including the Chief's. Though more often than not it was work that involved missing persons or the like, she had had her fair share of homicides, including the bodies of those laborers up in Sonoma County and that little girl they had found stuffed into the storm drain in Los Angeles.

But this case was beginning to get to her. And that was surprising. Because ever since that first story about her in the *National Enquirer* had started the flood of requests back in '71, after she had phoned in her premonition about the killer of the student nurses in Ohio, she had seen it all, every kind of crime, and all of it was distasteful.

Yet ... she wondered if she had been wise in picking this one, after all. There would be others in Santa Mara, other ways to help an old friend. A hit-and-run manslaughter, say. Or a gas station holdup, a liquor store shootout, a beating in the park. That sort of opportunity came up all the time.

But this.

There was, she couldn't help thinking, something truly nightmarish about it.

"So what were you getting at, Polly," said the Chief, taking a seat across from her at the interrogation table, "when you said there was another one?"

"Oh, there is," she said.

"Same M.O.? I mean —"

"I know what you mean," she said calmly. "Another body, female, buried in the same area. But he didn't use a gun this time. In fact, I'm not too clear on just how he did it. But she's in the same general location. You'll find her, I see it."

"Well, if there was one more unidentified on the list, we'll know about it soon enough. Meanwhile, I'd better get another team over to the Point. Is it our friend in the red shirt again?"

"Yes."

The Chief sighed and leaned back, like a man who has done an honest morning's work, and lit up one of the Viceroys. "Polly, I just don't know. I don't know how you do it."

"Neither do I, Jack," she said, reaching for the pack.

"Maybe I should say I don't know *why* you do it. I mean, what's in it for you? You know I can't pay more than your plane ticket — the Commission won't go for it. Of course I could pay you out of my own pocket —"

"Nonsense," she said. "I wouldn't hear of it." She

frowned. "How can you smoke these, Jack?" She broke off the filter. "It does have its rewards, though."

"What? Donations, that sort of thing?"

"Oh, some of the families try to pay me, but I send it back. And some money does come in the mail. And if it doesn't have a return address, I guess I have to do something with it, don't I?" She smiled and picked tobacco from her lip with a long red nail. "But it's not that much, really. Not as much as the magazines seem to think."

The Chief shook his head. "So. How about some lunch for now, Polly?" he said.

"Why certainly, Jack." She gave him a long stare. "As long as I'm here, I'm at your service."

"Right," said the Chief. He stood. "There's a coffee shop on the mall, or —"

"What's your office like?"

"I could have it sent over, sure. But —"

"I'd prefer it," she said. "That way we'll know as soon as anything breaks."

He studied her. "You're a pro, aren't you, Polly? A real pro."

"Why, thank you, kind sir. I guess I just like to be where the action is."

"You'll get your action, all right," he said. "There'll be fireworks all over the place when we get him. *If* we get him."

"Oh, we'll get him," she said. "I can promise you that."

The afternoon crept by.

Then, a few minutes after four o'clock, the Chief shouldered his way into his office and locked the door. He turned to find her still sitting there, dragging on an unfiltered cigarette.

"This one is going to be a tough nut to crack, Polly," he said. His voice was hoarse.

She waited.

He leaned over the chair, his heavy arms supporting his tired body. "How do you figure it?"

"Figure what?"

"We go through his apartment top-to-bottom — but there isn't a God damned thing, right? No bloody clothing, no muddy shoes, no diary, nothing. A big fat goose egg. So we're interviewing the people in the building, running the names in his little black book. But he's a smoothie, you know what I mean? One of those professor characters. Ronald Wilson Claiborn, Ph.D. Moustache, sideburns, you've seen the type. Lots of connections in the right places. Won't say word one till the ACLU gets here. The ACLU! Hell, he's gonna be talking false arrest, a press conference when he gets out, the whole bit." The Chief groaned. "Christ!"

"You're not going to cut him loose, are you, Jack." She said it as a statement.

There was an awkward pause.

"I can't hold him more than seventy-two hours, doll, you know that. Not unless we get another break."

"I'm sure this time, Jack," she said. "Don't look at me like that. What about the red shirt?"

"I'm not looking at you any way," he said wearily. "Yeah, we found the shirt. So what? The lab won't get anything. It's been to the cleaners at least once — still in the plastic bag. Do you know how many red Pendietons there are in Santa Mara?" He shook his head. "So what else do I have? The way things stand up now, I can't make a case. It's circumstantial. Or not circumstantial enough. Besides, no court in this country is going to swear in your testimony. I need this conviction, Polly."

Yes, she thought. So do I. How lucky for you, then, and for me, of course, that I'm able to give you just the kind of man you've secretly despised for so long: a college professor, an intellectual. The kind of suspect you've always wanted so badly to nail.

"I told you where to find the other body," she said with irritation.

His head continued to shake as he rested his huge buttocks on the edge of the desk. "Billy's team turned it up, all right."

"But what?"

"But we can't make the ID. It's too decomposed. Hell, we can't even make the dental charts."

"And why not?"

"Because we can't find the head."

"Okay, okay," she said sharply.

Circumstantial, she thought. I should have known. You want circumstantial? I'll give you circumstantial.

"Set up your tape recorder again, Jack. I'm going to give you what you need."

A body. The body of a woman. The nude body of a young woman. The body quivering under the eucalyptus trees as the head is taken from it.

"That's right," said the Chief, after she had told them. "Then what? What does he do with the knife, Polly? Hide it? Does he forget to wipe it off? Or drop something? Yeah, that would do fine. A button, keys — anything. And what about the gun from the first time? Try, baby. For God's sake, try!"

She let his voice slip away in the mist and peered deeper into the vision. A figure running at the edge of the scene, scudding frantically down an embankment slick with putrefying leaves. But that would do her no good now; she let go of the image.

"The apartment," she whispered, trying hard to get there. The pink apartment. Number six. She searched, allowing her mind to drift above the floor, above the rug like a disembodied eye. "Yes, I see ..."

The Chief breathed heavily.

"I see ..." She forced herself to explore the dark corners and hidden places, directed by memory, though it had been such a long time. Then she said, "Yes. There, in the closet."

"But we checked —"

"Behind the paperbacks ..." He used to do that years ago, toss his overshoes into the closet after a camping trip, and it was still there. "Mud. From his heels." The same kind? Yes, they would say that. They would be able to "prove" it somehow. Because they had to.

The Chief positioned the microphone closer to her. He held his breath.

"In ... the alley. Empty cartons. Not empty. Yes. I see ... a shirt." It was another Pendleton, the one he had been wearing when he cut himself on a fishing trip, and he had finally thrown it out. And it was red. The only color he ever bought. She had been safe in saying that. She hoped the blood type would match. With any luck it would.

"That's it, Polly! Talk to me, babe. We're almost home."

The tape recorder hummed in the small room. Her hands tightened on the arms of the chair. She stiffened, pressing forward. The sounds in the next office, the rumble of traffic on the other side of the barred windows became the roar of the earth as it buckled under the rains and began to move, disgorging its dead, but she fought it back. Her hands went to her ears.

"No," she said.

Then her hands fell to the table once more, her fingers twitching. Slowly she regained control.

"The car. Black. Under the floorboard. The mat. Look there. See ..."

"What, Polly?"

"Leaves." Yes. Only one, but it would have to do. A single eucalyptus leaf carried on his shoe from somewhere and knocked loose by the pedal, slivered there under the edge who knows how long ago. But it was the same kind. It would do.

There were more details, like the fishing knife that had cut him accidentally, in the tackle box of the boat locker at the harbor, stained with his own blood. Again she hoped it would turn out to be the same type as the girl's. But already she had the feeling; she knew. It always worked out.

Finally she lowered her head. When she raised it again, the office was alive with activity. The Chief was snapping his fingers, spitting orders into the phone, hustling his men out the door. She rubbed her eyes.

"You did it, doll," he said. He winked at her.

She rose unsteadily.

"You're not leaving yet," he said. He sounded surprised.

"I have to," she said. "I've got a plane to catch. To Denver. They need my help. A child was strangled there last month and they don't have any leads, none at all."

"Hold it right there," said the Chief.

He left the office for a moment. She heard a muffled conversation, the sound of a locker clanging open. She thought she felt the ground begin to shift under her feet, far beneath the floor and the concrete foundation of the building, but she pushed it out of her mind.

"Here you go." The Chief thrust a carton of Lucky Strikes into her hands. "You know you deserve a hell of a lot more," he told her. "And you know I know it, too. Don't you, babe?" He reached into his coat for a check. It was already made out. He tried to fold her fingers around it.

"You know me better than that, Jack," she said. She pushed his hand away.

They walked together down the hail.

"Don't you even want to see him?" said the Chief.

"Who?"

"The creep. Aren't you curious, at least? Or is it already over for you?"

She hesitated.

The Chief led her into a darkened room. When her eyes had adjusted she made out a row of seats, and a pane of glass that took up most of one wall. She reached for a cigarette with shaky fingers.

He stopped her hand. "Two-way mirror," he said.

She looked through to the man on the other side. He was seated at a table in a straight-backed chair. Tweed jacket, rust-colored wool tie loosened at the collar. He was being questioned by two detectives. His expression was serene and self-assured, as always. Even more confident than she remembered, in fact.

But that will change soon enough, she thought.

"That's him," said the Chief. "That's Claiborn"

Well, so long, Ronnie, she thought. Do you even

remember me? You'll probably never know. If you do find out, you should be grateful, for in a way I've saved you. I've stopped you from treating anyone else the way you treated me so long ago. In a sense I've helped you, more than you know, more than you'll ever know. In the darkness, she blew him a kiss.

She went back out into the hall. The Chief walked her to the lobby.

"I reckon it's so long, then, till next time," he said. "Can't truthfully say I hope to need you again, Polly. It's always good to see you, though, you know that. What's next for you now? After Denver, that is?"

She sorted through her purse for her notebook.

"Oh, there was a kidnapping back in Rochester," she said. "And that terrible business in Kansas. And then, let me see, there was that funny drowning down in Malibu. Have you heard about that? I don't know if I can schedule them all. Chances are I'll be out to the Coast to see you again soon enough. Just wait and see."

The police station was now busy with noisy activity, switchboards and teletypes banging away full force.

"Listen," he said, "I could call the press in for you — set it up in a few minutes. All it takes is a couple of phone calls. That way you'd at least get some publicity out of this." When she didn't say anything, he said, "But I guess you don't need it, do you? And knowing you, Poll, I'd guess you don't want it, either."

"Justice," she said, "is its own reward. That and being able to do a favor for an old friend ..."

She walked to the street. The night was coming fast. As she stood at the curb waiting for her police escort, she thought she saw a movement out of the corner of her eye. But it was only the persistence of the vision: a lonely figure scrabbling down a hillside, frightened by the sudden realization of what he had done. She saw him clearly now for only an instant, like the glimmer of the first star of evening that disappears when you stare too long at it.

He was young, a poor Mexican or Puerto Rican by the looks of him, and his trousers were filthy with mud as she had said. She had told the truth about that part. But that was all. He had no car waiting, no apartment to go to; his shirt was blue denim, though it was almost too wet and dirty to be sure. She wondered idiy where he was going. Did he know? Up or down the state, did it matter? He would be caught sooner or later for something else. That was always the way. As he turned to run, his ankles sinking deep into the mulch of the graveyard, she caught a fleeting glimpse of his eyes, dark and quick in an intelligent, utterly terrified face.

She closed her eyes, trying to shut it out.

When she opened them, a patrol car was pulling to a halt in front of her.

She reached for the handle. She was startled by how cold it was to her touch.

The young lieutenant climbed out to help her. He tipped his hat.

"Where to?" he said.

Where? Let's see. There's that bastard of a salesman in Denver, she thought. And there's my old teacher, retired and living in Rochester, And the boy who moved to Kansas, or at least he had been a boy then, like her in his teens when he had tried to rape her that night. And after that ...

She was aware of her hand on the door. The cold of the metal was seeping into her fingers, spreading up her goose-fleshed arm, grasping for her chest, seeking to grip her heart with a deathlike chill. She concentrated, focusing her attention. She snatched her hand away.

And then she felt the rumbling. She felt it first in her feet and then in her entire body. *My God,* she thought, *is it the whole street?*

"What ... what is that?" she asked the officer.

"Pardon, ma'am?"

Now the vision was upon her again, fiercer than ever this this time. She saw the gray clouds, the heavy soil bubbling and roiling and breaking up through the dark greenery, and then the long, glistening scratchings of the dead awash in the storm as they descended the hills. It was as if the world were being burst apart from within, from its most secret and hidden depths.

The officer was touching her, shaking her shoulder.

"Ma'am?" he was saying.

She forced the image to stop. *Now,* she thought. It grew fainter and faded. It seemed to take a long time. Too long.

"Wh-what? Oh, Billy. It was nothing, nothing at all. I thought I had forgotten something. I just had a bad moment there, that's all ..."

And she got into the car and rode without speaking all the way to the airport, waiting for the earth-moving machines to come in and finish it. But they never did.

Dennis Etchison

DAUGHTER OF THE GOLDEN WEST

At the school were three boys who were best friends. Together they edited the campus newspaper, wrote or appeared in plays from time to time, and often could be seen huddled together over waxed paper lunches, over microscopes in the biology lab, sometimes until dark, over desks leafed with papers most Saturdays, elbow to elbow with their English Department advisor, and even over the same clusters of girls gathered like small bouquets of poppies on the steps of the cafeteria, joking and conning and in general charming their way through the four long years.

Almost four years.

Don and Bob were on the tennis squad, Don and David pasted-up the Buckskin Bugler feature pages, Bob and David devised satirical skits for the annual Will & Prophecy Class Assemblies, and together they jockeyed for second, third and fourth positions in their graduating class—the first place was held inexplicably by one of those painted-smile, spray-haired secretary types (in fact she was Secretary of the Senior Class) named Arnetta Kuhn, and neither separately nor *en masse* could they dislodge, dissuade, distract, deflower or dethrone that irritating young woman from her destiny as Valedictorian, bent as she had been upon her goal since childhood, long before the boys had met, a target fixed in her mind as a stepping stone to a greater constelladon of goals which included marrying the most promising young executive in Westside Hills, whoever he might happen to be, and furnishing him and a ranch-style home yet to be built on South American Street with four dishwater-haired children and a parturient drawerful of Blue Chip Stamps. And so it went.

Until May, that is: the last lap of the home stretch.

Until Bob disappeared.

In the Formica and acetate interior of the mobile home in Westside Hills Court, Don of the thick black hair and high white forehead, lover of Ambrose Bierce and master of the sweeping backhand, and David, the high school's first longhair, collector of Marvel comics and articles on quantum physics, commiserated with Mrs. Witherson over cans of sugar-free cola (it was the only kind she had, now that Bob was gone), staring into their thumbnails and speaking softly in tones that were like a settling of throttled sighs over an as yet unmarked grave. It was a sad thing, surely, it was mysterious as hell, and most of all, each thought secretly, it was unfair, the most unfair thing he could have done.

The trophies, glassed certificates and commendations Bob had earned reflected around Mrs. Witherson, bending the dim, cold light into an aurora behind her drooped, nodding head.

"Maybe he ran off with a. With some kind of woman. The way his father did."

Instantly regretting it, a strange thing to say, really, Mrs. Witherson closed a shaking hand around the water glass and tipped it to her lips. The sherry wavered and clung, then evaporated, glistening, from the sides; she had taken it up again weeks ago, after the disappearance, and now the two were concerned about her as if by proxy. For Bob had told them, of course, of the way she had been for so long after the loss of his father. He had been too small to

62

remember him, but he had remembered the fuming glasses and shaking hands, he had said, and now his friends remembered them, too, though they did not speak of these things or even look up as she drank.

"I thought —" *Bob's father was killed in the war,* David started to say, but stopped, even without Don's quick glance and furtive headshake.

"He had. So much. Going for him." Bob's mother drained the glass, gazing into it, and David saw the tip of her slow, coated tongue lap after the odor of nonexistant droplets along the lip. "You all know that." And it was a larger statement than it sounded, directed beyond the trailer to include and remind them all, whoever needed to be reminded of the essential truth of it, herself, perhaps, among them.

They jumped, all three of them. The telephone clattered with an unnatural, banshee urgency in the closed rectangle of the trailer. The Melmac dishware ceased vibrating on the plastic shelf as Mrs. Witherson picked up the receiver. She took it unwillingly, distastefully, between the circle of thumb and finger.

David pushed away from the unsteady, floor-bolted table and chewed the inside of his mouth, waiting to catch Don's eyes.

"Mm-hm. Ye-es. I see."

It might have been an invitation to a Tupperware party. A neighbor whose TV set was on the blink. A solicitation for the PTA, which could have accounted for the edge in her voice. But it was not; it was not. They both knew it without looking at each other, and were on their feet by the aluminum screen door seconds before Mrs. Witherson, white-faced, dropped the receiver. It swung from the coiled cord, dipping and brushing the chill linoleum floor.

The lieutenant at the police station wrote out the address of the county morgue and phoned ahead for them. They drove in silence, pretending absorption in traffic lights. It was really not like the movies. An official in a wrinkled white smock showed them three 8 x 10's and there was not much talk, only a lot of nods and carefully avoided eyes and papers to be signed. Don stepped into a locked room and returned so quickiy that he must have turned on his heel the instant the sheet was lifted. During that brief moment and through the miles of neon interstices after David did not think of the photographs.

What was left of Bob had been found by a roadside somewhere far out of town.

And it was "just like the other two," the attendant said.

They drove and did not stop even when they were back in Westside. Don took corner after corner, lacing the town in smaller and smaller squares until each knew in his own time that there was nowhere to go and nothing to be said. David was aware of the clicking of the turn indicator and the faint green flickering of the light behind the dashboard. Until he heard the hand brake grind up. The motor still running. Without a word he got out and into his own car and they drove off in different directions.

David could not face his room. He hovered through the empty streets around his house for half an hour before his hands took over the wheel for themselves. He found himself in the parking lot of the Village Pizza Parlor. He drifted up next to Don's car and slipped inside, leaving the keys in the ignition.

Don was hunched to the wall, dialing the pay phone. David sidled over to a table in the corner and climbed onto the bench across from Craig Cobb, former star end for the Westside Bucks and Student Council football lobbyist.

"Hey, listen, Don told me about Bob and, hey, listen, I'm sorry."

David nodded and shuffled his feet in the sawdust.

Craig's lip moved over the edge of the frosted root beer. He probably wanted to pump David for details, but must have dimly perceived the nature of the moment and chose instead to turn his thick neck and scrutinize the player piano in the corner, now mercifully silent.

Don returned to the table.

"My mother's going over to stay with Mrs. Witherson

tonight," he said, sliding in next to Craig. Then, meeting David's eyes for the first time in hours, "Craig here tells me we ought to talk to Cathy Sparks."

They looked at each other, saying, *All right, we're in something now, and we're in it together, and we both know it,* and Craig glanced from one to the other and sensed that they were in something together, and that it was about their best friend who was dead and no one knew why, and he said, "R'lly. He went out with her, y'know."

That was wrong. Bob hadn't been going with anybody last semester. If he had, they would have known. Still, the way Don's eyes were fixing him, David knew there was more to hear.

Craig repeated the story. "No, see, it was just that weekend. Saturday." Right, that was the last time they had seen Bob. He had been working on that damned Senior History paper. "I was washing my car, right? And Robert pulls in next to me, the next stall, and starts rollin' up the windows and so I ask him, you know, 'Who're you takin' to the Senior Party?' An' he says he doesn't know yet, and so I say, 'Goin' to any good orgies tonight?' and he says, 'What d'you know about the new girl?' I guess, yeah, I think he said he gave her a ride home or something. I got the idea he was goin' over to see her that night. Like she asked him to come over or something. You know."

The new girl. The one nobody had had time to get close to, coming in as she had the last month or six weeks of school. A junior. Nobody knew her. Something about her. Her skin was oiled, almost buttery, and her expression never changed. And her body. Dumpy — no, not exactly; it was just that she acted like she didn't care about how she looked most of the time; she wore things that covered her up, that had no shape. So you didn't try for her. Still, there was something about her. She was the kind of girl nobody ever tried for, but if somebody asked somebody if he'd ever gotten anything off her, you would stop what you were doing and listen real close for the answer.

"So maybe you'll want to talk to her. She's the last one to see him. I guess." The football player, unmoving in his felt jacket, glanced nervously between them.

David stared at Don, and Don continued to stare back. Finally they rose together, scraping the bench noisily against the floor.

"Only thing is, she'll be pretty hard to find, prob'ly."

"Why's that?" asked David.

"I heard she moved away soon as the school year was over."

Later, driving home, taking the long way, thinking, David remembered the photographs. The way the body was mangled. Cut off almost at the waist. He tried, but this time he could not get it out of his mind.

So they did a little detective work the next day.

Bob's mother had not seen him after that Saturday morning, when he left for the library to work on his research paper. No one else had seen him after that, either. Except Craig. And maybe, just maybe, the girl.

So.

So the family name was in the phone book, but when they got there the apartment was up for rent. The manager said they had moved out the 12th, right after finals.

So they stopped by the school.

The Registrar's office was open for summer school and Mrs. Greenspun greeted them, two of her three favorite pupils, with a warmth undercut by a solicitous sadness of which she seemed afraid to speak. It was like walking into a room a second after someone has finished telling a particularly unpleasant story about you behind your back.

Yes, she had received a call, she said, a call asking that Cathy's grades be sent along to an out-of-town address.

"The young lady lives with her older sister, I take it," confided Mrs. Greenspun.

David explained that he had loaned her a book which she had forgotten to return.

"Of course," said Mrs. Greenspun maternally. And gave them the address.

It was in Sunland, a good hour-and-a-hall away.

David volunteered his old Ford. They had to stop once for directions and twice for water and an additive that did not keep its promise to the rusty radiator. In the heat, between low, tanned hills that resembled elephants asleep or dead on their sides under the sun, Don put down the term paper. They had picked it up from Mr. Broadbent, Bob's history teacher, and had put off turning it over to his mother. They had said they were going to read it but had not, sharing a vague unease about parting with the folder.

It was only the preliminary draft, with a lot of the details yet to be put in, but it was an unbelievable story.

"He was really into something strange," muttered Don, pulling moist hair away from the side of his face.

"I guess that means we can talk about it now."

"I guess," said Don. But his tone was flat and he kept watching the heat mirages rising up from the asphalt ahead.

"I've read something about it," pressed David. "It's pretty grim, isn't it." A statement.

"It's got to be the most horrible story I've ever read. Or the most tragic. Depending on how you look at it," said Don. "Both," he decided.

David felt subjects mixing. He was light in the head. He sucked on a bottle of Mountain Dew and tried to shift the conversation. "What did that guy at the coroner's office mean, do you think?"

"You mean —"

"I mean about the 'other two'." Suddenly David realized he had not changed the subject at all.

"Well, you remember Ronnie Ruiz and — what was the other one's name?"

David remembered, all right. Two others had disappeared, one a couple of weeks before Bob, the first a few weeks before that. A month or six weeks before the end of school. He had known what the attendant meant but had been carrying around a peculiar need to hear it confirmed. "Patlian, I think. The younger one, Jimmy Patlian's brother.

The junior. But I thought he ran off to join the Reserves."

"I don't know. It must have been him. Give me a swig of that shit, will you? Hey, how can you drink this?"

"I know, I know, my teeth'll fall out," said David, relieved to talk about something else. "But we always had it around the house when I was a kid. I guess you can be raised to like a thing, just like your parents' parents probably gave them the taste. Hard to put down."

"Sure, man, just keep telling yourself that until your stomach starts eating itself. Anyway, I know they found Ronnie Ruiz in some kind of traffic thing. Torn up pretty bad."

"The guy didn't even have a car, did he?"

"I don't — no, now that you bring it up. But they found him by some road somewhere. Maybe he got hit. The way I remember it, no one could identify him for sure for quite a while. Shit, man." He handed back the sweltering bottle. "This is shit."

"It's shit, all right," said David. "A whole lot of it."

"Cathy?"

"I remember you." The girl showed herself at the shadowed edge of the door, out of the blinding sun. "And you. I didn't think you'd bring anyone with you, when you called," she said to David, softly so that it was almost lost in the din of the freeway above the lot.

"This is Don. He —"

"I know. It's all right. My sister will be pleased."

The boys had worked out a scenario to ease her along but never got past side one. She had a quality of bored immobility which seemed to preclude manipulation, and a lack of assertiveness which made it somehow unnecessary.

They sat in three corners of the living room and made conversation.

She was not pretty. As their eyes mellowed to the heavily draped interior, her face began to reflect warm tones like the smooth skin of a lighted candle: oiled wax. She wore a loose, very old fashioned dress, high-necked, a ribboned cameo choker. As at school, though now the effect was in keeping with the close, unventilated room studded with fading, vignetted photographs and thin, polished relics of bone china. She moved without grace or style. She all but stood as she walked, all but reclined as she sat, inviting movement from others.

The afternoon passed. She drew them out, and they did not feel it happening.

Finally the ambience was broken momentarily. She left the room to refill their sweating glasses.

Don blinked. "There is something about that girl," he began measuredly, "and this place, that I do not like." He sounded nearly frightened about it, which was odd. "Does any of this remind you of anything?"

David rested his head against lace. His scalp was prickling. "Any of what? Remind me of what?"

When she reappeared with new iced teas, cooled with snowball-clumps of ice, Don had repositioned himself at the mantle. He fingered a discolored piece of an old mirror.

"How well did you know Bob Witherson, Cathy?" he asked, gazing into the glass as if for reflections of faces and events long past, something along the lines of a clue.

She paused a beat, then clinked the refreshments into their coasters. Unruffled, noticed David, trying to get a fix on her.

"I met Bobby at the library," she explained. "I saw the paper he was writing. We talked about it, and he asked me to help him. I invited him over for dinner. At my sister's."

As simple as that.

David had been sitting one way for so long, his eyes picking over the same curios, that he was beginning to experience a false gestalt. When Cathy sat again, he almost saw her sink back into the familiar shimmering outline that was etched on his retinas, the image of her sitting/lying in the overstuffed chair as she had for — how long? Hours? But this time she remained perched on the edge, as if in anticipation. David found himself focusing on details of her face: the full, moistened lips. And her body: the light pressure of her slim belly rising and falling to flutter the thin gingham dress. How much fuller, more satisfied she had looked when he first saw her, right after she came to Westside. Than the last time he had seen her, too, a couple of weeks before graduation. Now she seemed fragile, starved. She was watching him.

"These pieces must be very old," said Don from across the airless room. He lifted a fragment of a teacup. It was decorated in the delicate handiwork of another era, blue and red and purple flowers scrolled into the pure white ground surface of the chinaware.

David, watching Cathy watching him as he waited to make a move, resented the interruption.

"Yes." She spoke easily from another level, undistractible. "My great-great grandmother brought them with her from Springfield. In Illinois."

David inched forward.

"They came West, did they?" continued Don strangely, getting at something. "Would ... do you mind? I mean, I was wondering," he faltered, atypically, "where did they settle? I mean, where do you come from?"

"Sacramento, originally."

David rose. He crossed the room halfway. He stopped on a worn virgule in the carpet. Cathy's eyes opened wider to him. He was aware in a rush of the power assumed by someone who simply waits and asks no questions. But understanding it made it no less effective.

"Your sister has an interesting house," said David.

"You might like to see the rest," she offered cooly.

But Don was still busy formulating something and he would not let go. David had seen that expression before.

"Why," Don asked carefully, his words hanging like bright bits of dust in the air, "did Bob ask you to help him on his paper?" So he saw what was happening to David, saw it and recognized it and tried to push past it anyway. "Why *would* he?" he directed at David, as if the obvious reasons were not enough.

For once Cathy ignored a question. She got up and walked into the hallway, drawing it out as long as she could, aware of his eyes on her back. Perhaps she was smiling.

70

She turned. Out of Don's line of sight she said, "The parts you haven't seen yet are in here." And so saying she leaned forward, grasped the hem of her long dress and lifted it to the waist. She was naked underneath. Her eyes never left David.

The moment was unreal. She seemed to tilt before his eyes.

David moved toward the hall.

Don, thinking she was far into another room, launched a volley of words in a frantic stage whisper.

"We've got to get together on this," he said. And, "Think!" And, "I say her people came through Truckee in 18 — what. 1846." And, "David, what about it? What does that mean to you?" And, "That's why he wanted her help on the research. It's starting to add up. Does that make sense, Davey? Does it? Does it?!" And, "I don't know, it's crazy, but there's something more. What's the matter, you think it's something that scares me? Why should it? You think I'm fucking crazy? *Do you?*"

As David entered the bedroom the roar of the freeway gained tenfold, a charge of white sound in his ears. He thought she was saying something. He could not see her at first. Then a flurry of cloth and a twisting blur of white skin. Disjointedly he remembered Don as he had left him there in the darkening living room as the sun went down outside. Here in the bedroom it was almost completely dark — the east side of the house, the drapes thicker. Gradually his ears attuned to sounds closer than the churning traffic. Words Don had spoken in that choked whisper: *What about it? What about it?* Over and over like a ticking clock inside him. He felt his body flushed, feverish. People who live like this must be afraid of the cold. His eyes began to clear. He was aware of a slow, tangled movement about the edges of the room. Probably the curtains in the breeze. *Afraid of the cold.* He saw her now faintly like a fish in dark waters, under ice, sliding horizontally beneath him on the curve of the bed. He felt himself fevered, swelling. Her cold, damp fingers raised his shirt and found the hairs on his chest. She slipped under his belt, thumbed and pulled, straining the buckie. He heard his zipper winding open. Did he? The shapes moving against the walls in the breeze. Hushed swishing sounds. The freeway? Closer, closer. *There was no breeze.* "Are you hungry?" she asked and then laughed a kind of laugh he had never heard before. She slid back and forth under him, spreading her fishbelly-white legs wider. He moved to her, his body trembling. "No." Her voice. Of course. Of course. "First let me eat you." She said it. All right. All right? In the protracted second as she sat up, as she gripped his waist like a vise, sudden images flashed to mind: words written in the dark and illuminated from within. They came in a surge, crowded in on him. My sister will be pleased, she had said. What sister? He laughed. Almost laughed. Now he was sure of the presence of others in the room. They undulated along the walls. How many? This is crazy. She had sisters, yes, that was it, sisters, from Sacramento, descended from Truckee and the great trek to Sutter's Fort. "Oh my God," he said aloud, his voice cracking. And in the next second everything, all of it came at once. As he felt her mouth enfold him he saw Bob with her, and as her lips tightened he saw Bob in the photographs, and as her teeth scraped hungrily over him, drawing him deeper into her, he saw Bob's body, torn, consumed almost to the waist, and as the teeth bit down for the first time, bit down and would not be released, grinding sharply together, it all exploded like a time bomb and he heard his scream off the walls and the freeway's pulse, above her house, the road where young men were tossed afterwards like so much garbage and the sound of the sighing women as he passed into unconsciousness and Don burst confused into the room with the second draft from her desk where he had found it and before he could form an answer or even another question about Bob's paper on the Donner Party and her strange knowledge of it her sisters swooped from the corners where they had been crouched in waiting and then they were upon him, too.

THE PITCH

The third floor came down to meet him.

As far as he could see, around a swaying bunch of sphagnum moss that was wired to one of the brass fire nozzles in the sound-proofed ceiling, a gauntlet of piano legs staggered back in a V to the Kitchen Appliance Department like sullen, waiting lines of wooden soldiers. C-Note shuddered, then cursed as the toe guard clipped the rubber soles of his wedgies.

He stepped off the escalator.

He turned in a half-circle, trying to spot an opening.

A saleswoman, brittle with hairspray, dovetailed her hands at her waist and said, "May I help you, sir?"

"No, ma'am," said C-Note. He saw it now. He would have to move down alongside the escalator, looking straight ahead, of course, pivot right and weave a path through the pink and orange rows of the Special Children's Easter Department. There. "I work for the store," he added, already walking.

"Oh," said the saleswoman dubiously. "An employee! And what floor might that be? The, ah, Gourmet Foods on One?"

If it had been a joke, she abandoned her intention at once. He swung around and glared, the little crinkles fanning out from his eyes, deepening into ridges like arrows set to fire on her. Her make-up froze. She took a step back.

A few women were already gathering listlessly near the demonstration platform. Just like chickens waiting to be fed. Ready. All angles and bones. *May I help you, sir?* I'll plump them up, he thought, swinging a heavy arm to the right as he pushed past a pillar. A small ornament made of pipe cleaners and dyed feathers hooked his sleeve. He swung to the left, shaking it off and heading between tables of rough sugar eggs and yellow marshmallow animals.

They looked up, hearing his footsteps. He considered saying a few words now, smoothing their feathers before the kill. But just then a sound pierced the Muzak and his face fisted angrily. It was *Chopsticks*.

He ducked backstage through the acetate curtain.

"They don't even notice," he wheezed, disgusted.

"Why, here he is," said the pitchman, "right on time." Seated on a gold anodized dining room chair borrowed from the Furniture Department, he was fooling with the microphone wired around his neck and waiting blankly for the next pitch. "All set to knock 'em dead, killer? What don't they notice?"

"They don't notice my hand goin' in their pocketbooks in about fifteen minutes." C-Note sprawled over the second chair, also upholstered in a grained vinyl imprinted with lime-green daisies.

"Ha ha! Well, you just rest your dogs for now," said the pitchman. He spooled out a length of black plastic tape and began dutifully winding another protective layer around the microphone's coat hanger neckpiece.

C-Note saw that all was in ready: several cartons marked Ace Products, Inc., barricaded either side of the split curtain and behind the pitchman, leaned against two large suitcases, were lumpen bags of potatoes, a pried-open crate of California lettuce and a plastic trash can liner brimming over with bunched celery and the wilted cowlick tops of fat hybrid carrots. C-Note flexed his fingers in preparation, turned one wrist up to check his watch and pulled a white-gloved hand through his lank hair. He was not worried; it would not fall in his eyes, not now, not so long as he did not have to lean forward on a stool over another scale. Sometimes he had thought they would never end. Up and down, down and up.

"We got fifteen units out there," said the pitchman,

"another forty-eight in the box here. I don't think you'll have to touch 'em, though. The locations we do our best is the discount chains. You know."

"Sure," C-Note lied, "I know."

"These *ladies* —" He overlaid the word with a doubtful emphasis. "— They're all snobs, you know?" The pitchnian cut the tape and then paused, eyeing him as he pared dirt from under his fingernails with the vegetable knife.

C-Note stared at the man's hands. "You want to be careful," he said.

"Check, kid. You got to slant it just right. But you can sell anything, can't you? You talked me into it. I believe you."

That was what C-Note had told him. He had come up to the platform late yesterday, hung around for a couple of sets and, when the pitchnian had scraped off the cutting board for the last time and was about to pack up the rest of the units in the big suitcases and carry them out to the station wagon, he had asked for a job. *You want to buy one? Then don't waste my time.* But C-Note had barged through the curtain with him and picked up a unit, covering one of the kitchen chairs as if it had always been his favorite resting place. As he had done just now. And the pitch. The pitch he auditioned was good, better even than the original mimeo script from Ace. If he pitched as well out there today in front of the marks, the head pitchnian just might earn himself a bonus for top weekiy sales. Of course, C-Note would never know that. The pitchman had agreed to pay him cash, *right out of my own pocket,* for every sale. And how would C-Note know how much commission to expect? He would not bother to go to the company, not today and not next week, because that would mean W-2s, withholding — less take-home. And the new man looked like he needed every dime he could lay his hands on. His white-gloved hands.

"Here you go," said the pitchman. "I'll hold onto your gloves. Shake out a little talcum powder. That way you won't go droppin' quarters."

"The gloves," said C-Note, "don't come off." And the

way he said it told the pitchman that he considered the point neither trivial nor negotiable.

The pitchman watched him bemusediy, as if already seeing juice stains soaking into the white cloth. He stifled a laugh and glanced aside, as though to an audience: *Did you catch that?*

"Well, it's two o'clock, pal. I'm goin' up to the cafeteria. Be back in time to catch your act. You can start, uh, on your own, can't —?"

"Take it easy," said C-Note, waiting.

"Don't worry, now. I'm not gonna stick you with no check. Ha ha. Cash!" He patted his hip pocket. "Not every demonstrator's that lucky, you know."

"I appreciate it. But I'm not worried about the money."

"Yeah." The pitchnian handed him the neck microphone. "Sure." He looked the new man over again as if trying to remember something more to ask him, tell him. "Check," and he left, looking relieved to be leaving and at the same time uneasy about it, a very curious expression.

C-Note left the microphone on the chair and set to work on the units. He had to prepare them and these few minutes would be his only chance. If the pitchman had not volunteered to go to lunch, C-Note would have had to beg off the next demonstration and remain backstage while his boss pitched out front in order to get to them in time. He tightened his gloves and dug his fingertips into the big Ace carton and ripped the cardboard. They did not hurt at all anymore; he was glad of that, in a bitter sort of way.

"... And today only," droned C-Note, "as a special advertising premium from the manufacturer, this pair of stainless steel tongs, guaranteed never to rust, just the thing for picking baby up out of the bathtub ..."

He lifted a potato from the cutting board and plunked it ceremoniously into the waste hole. Most of the ladies giggled.

"That's right, they're yours, along with the Everlast glass knife, the Mighty Mite rotary tool, the Lifetime orange juicer *and* the fruit and vegetable appliance complete with five-year written warranty and two interchangeable surgical steel blades, all for the price of the VariVeger alone. If you all promise to go home and tell your friends and neighbors about us, extend our word-of-mouth. Because you will not find this wonder product on the shelves of your stores, no ma'am, not yet. When you do, next fall sometime, the new, improved VariVeger alone will list for a price of seven dollars and ninety-five cents. That's seven ninety-five for the shredder, chopper and julienne potato maker alone. You all remember how to operate this little miracle, don't you, so that you'll be able to put it to work on your husband's, your boyfriend's, your next door neighbor's husband's dinner just as soon as you get home tonight?"

More laughter.

"Just crowd in close as you can now, 'cause this is the last time I'm going to be demonstrating this amazing ..."

"Say, does that thing really work?"

"Three years of kitchen testing ..." C-Note saw that it was the head pitchman, watching from the aisle, a sporting smirk on his lips. "Three years of testing by the largest consumer laboratory ..."

There was something else.

Distracted, he let his voice roll off for a brief moment, heard the reverberation replaced by the dull din of milling shoppers, the ringing of cash registers and the sound of a piano playing on the other side of the Special Children's Easter Department. He hesitated, his teeth setting and grinding. Why wouldn't she let him stop? He hovered over the soggy cutting board, waiting for the sharp crack of the ruler on the music rest, just missing his knuckles.

A gnarled hand reached up, grasping for a VariVeger. C-Note snapped to.

"Just another minute, ma'am, and I'll be handing out the good-will samples. If you'll just bear with me, I'm sure you'll go away from this store feeling ..."

And so on and on. He peeled a potato, set it on the grid of the VariVeger and slammed his hand down on the safety guard handle. Dozens of slim, pallid, finger-like segments appeared underneath. A susurrus of delight swept the crowd.

"No need to hold back — the patented safety grip bar makes it for sure you won't be serving up finger stew tonight!"

Then he took up the Mighty Mite, needled it into a radish and rotated the blade, holding to the protective finger guard. And a good thing, too: without that tiny ridge of aluminum the blade would continue turning right down through glove, finger and jointed bone. Five seconds later he pulled the radish apart in an accordion spiral.

"Here's just the thing for that mother-in-law you thought you'd never impress!"

Oohs and ahhs. Nothing worked like a non sequitur.

He diced onions, he ripple-cut potato chips, lateral, diagonal and criss-cross, he sliced blood-red tomatoes into inflationary slips —

"This is one way to stretch that food bill to cover the boss, his wife, your in-laws, your husband and all sixteen screaming kids!"

— he squeezed gouts of juice from a plastic spout like a magician with a never-empty lotta, he slivered green beans and cross-haired a turnip into a stiff blooming white flower. He shredded lettuce head after head, he riced more potatoes, he wavy-edged a starchy-smelling mound of French fries, he chopped cabbage, he separated a cucumber into a fleshy green Mobius strip, he purled twists of lemon peel, he segmented a carrot, grated another, then finished by describing the Everlast glass knife, stacking the packages into a protective wall in front of him. You know. You know what he said. And he gave the signal and the money came forth and he moved forty-three unit combinations at a price less than one-half of the fanciful manufacturer's retail, the bills folded between his fingers like Japanese paper water flowers, blooming and growing in the juices as his gloves became green, green as Christmas trees made of dollars.

He scraped the garbage into a hole, mopped his forehead, put away twenty unsold packages, stripped off his plastic apron, unplugged the mike and departed the platform.

Just as he was about to peel the drenched gloves from his hands, the head pitchman appeared at the slit in the curtain.

C-Note left his gloves on.

The pitchman flashed his hand forward, then thought better of it.

"Hell of a salesman," he announced.

"We thank you," said C-Note. "But —"

"Don't let it go to your head, though."

"No, sir. I got —"

"Hell of a salesman. But what the hell was that business with the knife?"

"I sold the knife. 'Long with the rest of the package. Isn't that all right, sir? But if you don't mind, I got to —"

"But you didn't *demonstrate* the knife. What's with that? You afraid you're gonna cut yourself or —"

C-Note's sharp eyes nailed him where he stood.

"If you don't mind, I got to go now." He started for the curtain, head down. "I mean, this gut of mine's startin' to eat itself. If you don't mind. Sir. If you think I earned my lunch."

"Hell yes, you earned it, boy." The pitchman put a foot up on the kitchen chair. His toe brushed the carton, the one with the torn-open top. "Hey, wait a minute."

C-Note drew back the curtain.

"Look, you want your money or don't you?"

C-Note turned back.

"Ha ha." The pitchman unfolded some money. C-Note took it without counting, which made the pitchman stare. "Hell of a salesman," he muttered, smiling crookedly. He watched the heavyset man leave.

"Kid must have to take a hell of a leak," the pitchman said to himself. It was only after he had counted and stacked the limp piles of bills in the money box, counted the units, shaken his head and paced the floor several times, lost in some ambitious vision, that he noticed the torn-up carton. "Hell of a salesman," he said again, shaking his head with pleasure. He poked around inside, counting the reserve. Cutting his finger on something, he drew it back with a grimace and stuck it in his mouth. "Well goddam," he said slowly, patiently, pulling up the crease in his trousers and seating himself before the carton from which, he now realized, unpackaged units had been inexplicably switched, "what in the name of the ..." *goddam holy hell do we have here?* he might have said.

C-Note hurried for the back stairs. On the landing he stopped and looked at his hands. They were trembling. Still moist, they resembled thick, mushy clumps of pseudopodia. Loosening the fingers one by one, he eased the gloves off at last.

His fingers quivered, fat and fishbelly-white. The tips were disfigured by a fine, shiny line. They had healed almost perfectly, sewn back right afterwards, in the ambulance; still, the fusion was not quite perfect, the ends angled out each slightly askew from the straight thrust of the digits. No one would notice, probably, unless they studied his hands at close range. But the sight of them bothered him.

He braced himself, his equilibrium returning. He swallowed heavily, his breath steadying, his heart leveling out to a familiar regular tattoo. There was no need to panic. They would not notice anything out of the ordinary, not until later. Tonight, perhaps. At home.

He recognized the feeling now as exhilaration. He felt it every time.

Too many steps to the ground floor. He turned back, stuffing the gloves into his coat pocket, and re-entered the store.

He passed quickly through the boundaries of the Kitchen Appliance Department. Mixers. Teflon ware. Beaters, spoons, ladles, spatulas, hanging like gleaming doctors' tools. If one were to fall it would strike the wood, making him jump, or smack the backs of his hands, again and again. One of them always had, every day. Some days a spoon, other days something else, depending on what she had been cooking. Only one day, that last day, had she been scoring a ham; at least it had smelled like a ham, he remembered, even after so many years. That day it had been a knife.

The Muzak was lilting, a theme from a movie? Plenty of strings to drown out the piano, if there was one. He relaxed.

The women had somnambulated aimlessly from the demonstration platform, their new packages pressed reas-suringly to their sides, moving like wheeled scarecrow mannequins about the edges of the Music Department. From here it was impossible to differentiate them from the saleswoman he had met there, by the pianos. She might have been any one of them.

He passed the platform and jumped onto the escalator. The rubber handrail felt cool under his grip. Hastily he pulled a new pair of white gloves from his inside pocket and drew them on.

At the first floor, on his way out to the parking lot, he decided to detour by the Candy Department.

"May I help you, sir?"

Her hands, full and self-indulgent, smoothed the gener-ous waist of her taut white uniform.

"A pound-and-a-half of the butter toffee nuts, all right, sweets?"

The salesgirl blushed as she funneled the fragrant candy into a paper sack. He saw her name badge: *Margie.* There was nothing about her that was sharp or demanding. She would be easy to please — no song and dance for her. He tipped her seventy-five cents, stroking the quarters into the deep, receptive folds of her soft palm.

He tilted the bag to his mouth and received a jawful of the tasty sugared nuts.

At the glass door he glanced down to see why the bag did not fit all the way into his wide trouser pocket. Then he remembered.

He withdrew one of the parts he had removed back-stage and turned it over, fingering it pleasurably as he waddled into the lot. It was a simple item, an aluminum ring snapped over a piece of injection-molded plastic. It glinted in the afternoon sunlight as he examined it. A tiny safety guard, it fit on the vegetable shredder just above the rim that supported the surgical steel blades. A small thing, really. But it was all that would prevent a thin, angular woman's fingers from plunging down along with cucumber or potato or soft, red tomato. Without it, they would be stripped into even, fresh segments, clean and swift, right to the bone. He slipped it back into his pocket, where it dropped into the reservoir of other such parts, some the little safety wheels from the vegetable garnisher, some the protective bars from the Mighty Mite rotary tool. But mostly they were pieces from the VariVeger, that delightful invention, the product of three years of kitchen testing, the razor sharp, never-fail slicer and stripper, known the world over for its swift, unhesitating one-hand operation.

He kept the bag in his hand, feeding from it as he walked on across the parking lot and down the block, losing himself at once in the milling, mindless congestion of Easter and impatient Mother's Day shoppers.

YOU CAN GO NOW

1.

The receiver purred in his hand.

He glanced around the bedroom, feeling as if he had just awakened from a long, dreamless sleep.

A click, then recorded music. He had been placed on hold. There was something he was trying to remember. Everything seemed to be ready, but —

"Thank-you-for-waiting-good-afternoon-Pacific-Southwest-Airlines-may-I-help-you?"

He told the voice about his reservation; he was sure he had one. Would she —

Yes. Confirmed.

He thanked her and hung up.

Wait. What was the flight number? He must have written it down — yes. It was probably in his wallet.

He bent over the coat on the bed, feeling for the slim leather billfold. There, in the breast pocket. He fumbled through business cards, odd papers, credit plates.

No.

But no matter. He would find out when he got there.

Still, there was *something*.

He pulled out the drawer in the nightstand, under the phone, and started poking around, not even sure of what he was looking for.

He found a long, unmarked envelope, near the bottom. He took it and held it tightly as he slipped the coat on, then put it into the inside pocket while he felt with his other hand for the keys. He patted his outer pockets, but they were not there.

Head down, he left the room.

His bags were stacked neatly by the wall of the foyer, but the keys were not there. He paced through the living room, the kitchen, checking the tables.

He went back to the bedroom, eyes down.

There.

By the door. The key ring was wedged by the bottom edge, between the door and the pile of the carpet, as though it had been flung or kicked there.

He picked it up, walked to the front door, lifted his bags, and went out to the car.

It was still early afternoon, so the freeway would be a clear shot most of the way.

He switched off the air conditioning — who had left it on? — and rolled down the window, stretching out. The seat was adjusted wrong again, damn it, so he had to grope for the lever and push with his feet, struggling to seat the runner back another notch.

He connected through to the San Diego Freeway, made the turn and tried to unwind the rest of the way. He sampled the radio, but it was only more of the same: back scratchings about love or the lack of it and the pleasure or the pain it brought or might bring; maybe, could be, possibly, for sure, always, never, too soon, not soon enough, in the wrong rain or the wrong style. *Wrong, wrong.* He flicked it off.

The airport turnoff would be corning up.

He flexed his arm, checking his watch. But it had stopped. The face was spattered with dry, flaking paint, so it would have been hard to read the numbers, anyway.

He toed the accelerator until he was moving five miles over the speed limit, then ten.

He was glad to have made such good time; a few extra minutes would mean a drink first, maybe two —

It was funny. The car ahead, at the foot of the ramp. The back-up lights were on, but not the brake lights. He did not slow, because it meant that the signal at the intersection would be —

Headlights. They were headlights.

Headed directly at him.

You can go now, said a voice.

He leaned on the horn, but then there was the heavy, bone-snapping impact and everything was driven into him with such force that the horn stayed on, bleating like a siren, whether or not he would have wanted it to or would even have thought of it or of anything, of anything else at all.

2.

He was late getting to LAX, so he swung at once into the western parking lot, hoofed it over to the PSA building and sloughed his bags through the metal detector without stopping at the flight information desk. A couple of quick questions later, a hostess in a Halloween-colored uniform was pointing him toward the boarding tunnel, and then another was ushering him onto the plane and back to the smoking section.

He stashed his bags and found himself in a seat on the aisle, next to a pregnant woman and two drugged-looking hyperactive children. They continued to squirm, but slowly, as though underwater, as he tugged at the seat belt, trying to dislodge the oversized buckle from beneath his buttocks.

A double vodka and two cigarettes later, he was halfway to Oakland and swinging inland away from the silvery tilt of the sea. He drained the ice against his teeth and snared the elbow of a stewardess.

Another?

Well, the bottles were all put away, but — yes. Of course.

Of course.

The smaller child was busy on the floor in front of the seat, trying to tear out the pages of a washable cloth picture book about animals who wore gloves and had one-syllable names. The child had already stripped the airline coloring book, the oxygen mask instruction card and the air sickness bag into piles of ragged chits. Now, however, he dropped his work and wobbled to his feet, straining to clamber up the seat and under his mother's smock.

But the mother was absorbed in the counting and recounting of empty punch cups — one, two, three, see? one, two three — over and over, for the older child, who was working with all his might to slide out from under his seat belt. He would flatten like a limbo dancer until his shoes touched the floor and his knees buckled; then the mother would reach down, hoist him back up and begin counting the cups for him again.

"One, two, three, see? Why don't you try, Joshua?"

Ignored, the smaller child twisted like a bendable rubber doll and, sucking the ink off two fingers, watched the man across from him.

Who looked away. He was, mercifully, beginning to feel something from the double: a familiar ease, faint but unmistakable. He folded his hands, cold against each other, and tried to unwind while there was still time. He caught a glimpse out the window of farmlands sectioned like the layers of a surgical operation, beyond the flashing tip of the wing.

The child followed his eyes. "Break-ing," the child announced.

Idly he watched the wing swaying slowly as it knifed through the air currents. He remembered seeing the wing moving up and down like that on his first flight, how he worried that it might break off until someone had explained to him about expansion and contraction and allowances for stress.

"What's breaking?" said the mother. "Nothing's break-ing, Jeremiah. Look, look what Mommy's ..."

The stewardess reappeared. She rattled the plastic serving tray, bending over his lap with the drink.

He reached into his back pocket for his wallet.

"Want more punch!" said the older child.

"More punch?" asked the stewardess.

The wallet wasn't there. He remembered. He reached inside his coat.

He felt a long envelope, and the billfold. He removed both, peeled off two bills and laid them on the tray.

"Break-ing!" said the smaller child.

At that moment a shadow passed over the tray and the stewardess's wet fingers. He glanced up.

Outside, heavy strands of mist had begun to drift above the wings, temporarily blocking the sun. Looking down, he saw the black outline of the plane passing over the manicured rectangles of land.

Suddenly, sharply, the plane dropped like an elevator falling between floors. Then just as suddenly it stopped.

"Looks like we might be hitting some turbulence," he said. "Sure you've got a pilot up there?"

His attention returned to the window. Now darker clouds dotted the view, turning the window opaque so that he saw a reflection of his own face within the thick glass.

He heard a voice say something he did not understand.

"What?" he said.

"I said, that's funny," said the stewardess, "like an open grave."

A flash of briliiant light struck outside, penetrating the cloud bank. She stopped pouring the drink. He looked up at her, then at the tray. He noticed that her hands were shaking.

Then a dull, muffled sound from the back of the plane. Then a series of jolts that rattled the bottle against the lip of the glass. He thought he heard a distant crackling, like ants crawling over aluminum foil. Then the quick, shocking smell of smoke wafted up the aisle.

"Oh my God," whispered the stewardess hoarsely, "we've been —"

"I know," he said, strangely calm, "I know," *with tears of blood I tell you I know.*

The tray, ice and drink went flying, and then they were falling, everything falling inward and children, pillows, oxygen masks, bottles, the envelope he still clutched stupidly in his hand, the whole thing, the plane and the entire world were falling, falling and would not, could not be stopped.

The Dark Country   **87**

3.

It was dusk as he drove into the delta, and the river, washed over with the memory of the dying red eye of the sun, seemed to be reflecting a gradual darkening of the world.

He wound down the windows of the rented car, cranking back the wind wings so that he could feel the air. The smell of seed crops and of the rich, silted undergrowth of the banks blew around him, bathing him in the special dark parturience of the Sacramento Valley.

He had been away too long.

And soon he would be back, away for a time from the practices of the city, which he had come to think of more and more lately as the art of doing natural things in an unnatural way — something he was afraid he had learned all too weil. But now, very soon, he would be back on the houseboat; for a while, at least.

He did not know how long.

He would anchor somewhere near The Meadows. He would tie up to that same tree in the deep, still water, near the striped bass hole, hearing the lowing of cattle from behind the clutch of wild blackberry bushes on shore ...

And this time, he dared himself, he might not go back at all. Not, at least, for a long, long time.

He drove past the weathered, century-old mansions left from the gold days, past the dirt roads marked only by rural mailboxes, past the fanning rows of shadowy, pungent trees, past the collapsing wooden walkways of the abandoned settlement towns, past the broad landmark barn and the whitewash message fading on its doors, one he had never understood:

HIARA PERU RESH.

He geared down and took the last, unpaved mile in a growing rush of anticipation. Rocks and eucalyptus pods rained up under the car, the wheel jerking in his hands, the shocks and the leaf springs groaning and creaking.

Then he saw a curl of smoke beyond the next grove and caught the warm smell of catfish frying over open coals. And he knew, at last, that he was nearing the inlet, the diner and the dock.

He braked in the gravel and walked down the path to the riverbank. He heard the lapping of the tide and the low, heavy knocking of hulls against splintered pilings. Finally he saw the long pier, the planks glistening, the light and dark prows of cabin cruisers rocking in their berths, the dinghies tied up to battered cleats, their slack, frayed ropes swollen where they dipped into the water, the buoys bobbing slowly, the running lights of a smaller, rented houseboat chugging away around the bend, toward Wimpy's Landing.

The boards moved underfoot as he counted the steps, head down, and he smiled, reminding himself that it would take a few hours to regain his sea legs. He reached the spot, a few yards from the end of the docking area, where he knew the *Shelley Ann* would be waiting.

He tried to remember how long it had been. Since the spring. Yes, that was right, Memorial Day weekend. Sometimes friends rode him about paying for the year-round space—why, when he used her only a few times each year? Even Shelley had begun talking that way in the last few weeks. *Cut your losses on that albatross!* She had actually said that. But at times like this, coming to her after so many months, he forgot it all. It felt like coming home. It always did.

He looked up.

The space was empty.

His eyes darted around the landing, but she was nowhere that he could see.

Unless — of course. She had been moved. That was it. But why? His boat had never been assigned any other stall for as long as he had owned her. Something had happened, then. But there had been no long distance call, no word in the mail; Old John would not be one to hide anything as serious as an accident. Would he?

He took a few steps, his hands in his back pockets, scanning the river in both directions.

He could just make out the diner/office/tackle shop through the trees. A dim light was burning behind the peeling wooden panes.

Yes. Old John would know. Old John would be able to tell him the story, whatever it was.

Which was the trouble. Knowing him, it would take an hour, two. A beer, three beers, maybe even dinner. The lonely old man would not let him go with a simple explanation, of that he was sure.

And now he found he could think only of the *Shelley Ann*. He had waited and he had planned and he had come all this way, and at the moment nothing else seemed to matter. He needed to feel her swaying under him, rocking him. Now, right now.

Then. Everything. Would be. All right.

He stepped off the end to the bank, peering under the covered section of the landing, even though he knew that his boat would have been too large to clear the drooping canvas overhang.

He crouched at the edge, feeling suddenly very alone. The river smelled like dead stars, He watched the water purl gently around the floats and echo back and forth over the fine sand. A few small bubbles rode the surface, and a thin patina of oil shone with mirror-like luminescence under the dimming sky, reflecting a dark, swirling rainbow.

No stars were visible yet. In fact, the sky above the trees grew more steely as he watched.

He looked again at the water. He fingered a chip of gravel and tossed it. It made a plunking sound and settled quickly, and as it disappeared he found that he was straining to follow it with his eyes all the way down to the bottom.

He reached into his coat for a cigarette. His hands were still cold, and growing colder.

He felt the cigarette case and drew it out, along with something else.

He pushed a cigarette into his lips and stared at the

envelope. It had no name and address on it. He couldn't remember —

He opened it, slipped out a neatly folded sheet of bond paper, unfolded it.

The leaves of the trees near him rustled, and then a light breeze strafed the water, tipping it with silver.

Still crouching, he fired up the lighter, lit the cigarette and squinted, trying to make out the words. It was written in careful longhand, a letter or — no. Something else.

He read the title.

The paper began to make a tapping sound. He held out his hand. Rain had started to fall, a light rain that danced on the river and left it glittering. As he blinked down at the paper, more drops hit the page. The ink began to run, blurring before his eyes.

The lighter became too hot to hold. He snapped it shut and stood. He heard the rain talking in the trees, on the canvas tarpaulin, on the struts of the rotting pier.

His legs were cramped. He made a staggering step forward. His shoes sloshed the water. He stepped still further, led by the swinging arc of his cigarette tip in the darkness, until the rain found the cigarette and extinguished it.

He dropped it and moved forward, ankle-deep in the river. Is she really there? he thought.

Then he waded out into the low tide, the rain striking around him with a sound like musical notes, the melting paper still gripped in his hand, trailing the water.

4.

Dazed, he glanced around the bedroom.

The receiver was in his hand. By now the plastic had become quite warm against his palm. He stared at it for a moment, then returned it to his ear.

He heard recorded music.

Click.

"Thank-you-for-waiting-good-afternoon-Pacific-Air-lines-may-I-help-you?"

There was something he wanted to tell her. He had

been trying hard to remember, but —

His eyes continued to roam the lower half of the room. Then he spotted the keys, the car keys, wedged between the bottom edge of the door and the pile of the carpet, as though they had been flung or kicked there with great force.

It started to come back to him. Shelley had done it. She had thrown the key ring with all her strength, a while ago. Yes. That had happened.

He raised his head at last, rubbed his neck.

And saw her, there on the other side of the bed.

She lay with eyes closed, hands at her sides, fingers clutching the bedspread.

He didn't want to disturb her. He modulated his voice, cupping the mouthpiece with his hand.

He told the maddeningly cheerful voice on the phone — it reminded him of a Nichiren Shoshu recruiter who had buttonholed him on the street once — to cancel one reservation. His wife was not ready, would not be ready on time.

Yes. Only one. That's right. Thank you.

He hung up.

He lifted the phone and replaced it on the nightstand.

On the bed, where the phone had been, was an envelope.

He picked it up.

It was empty.

There was a sheet of paper on the floor, where Shelley had crumpled and thrown it. That was right, wasn't it?

He smoothed it out on his knee.

It was written in a very careful, painstaking longhand, much more legible than his own. He started to read it.

At the end of the first stanza he paused.

Yes, it was something Shelley had found — no, she had had it all along, saved (hidden?) in her drawer in the nightstand. She had taken it out earlier this morning, or perhaps it had been last night, and had shown it to him, and one of them had become angry and crumpled it onto the floor. That was how it had started.

He read it again, this time to the end.

(1)
brown hair
curling smile
shadowed eyes
the line of your lips ...
hair tangled
over me

(2)
warm skin
tender breasts
your mouth and
sweet throat ...
hair moist
under me

(3)
there will be more
my eyes tell your eyes
than love of touch
face lost in my face ...
do you know what lives
between our breathing palms?

(4)
twisted hair
seashell ear
soft sounds
stopped by my chest ...
dark eyes sleep
while I speak to your heart

He turned to his wife.

It was true; she was beautiful. Whoever had written those words had loved her. He studied her intently until he began to feel an odd sense of dislocation, as if he were seeing her for the first time.

He looked again at the paper.

At the bottom of the page, following the last stanza, there was a name.

It was his own.

And in the corner, a date: almost fifteen years ago.

Quietly, almost imperceptibly, he began to cry.

For so much had changed over the years, much more than handwriting. He did not love her now, not in any traditional sense; instead, he thought, there was merely a sense of loving that seemed to exist somewhere between her and his mind.

As he sat there, he forced his eyes to trace the lines of her body, her face: the shrug of her sholders, the sweep of her long, slender neck, the surprisingly full jaw and yet the almost weak point of the chin, the slight lips, the sad curve at the corners of her mouth, the smooth, even shade of her skin, the narrow nose, the nearly parallel lines that formed the sides of her small face, the close-set eyes, the thin and almond-shaped lids and delicately sketched lashes, the worried cast of her forehead and the baby-fine wisps at the hairline, the soft down that grew near her temples, the fuller curls that filled out a nimbus around her head, the hair bunched behind her neck, the ends hard and stiff now where the dried brown web had trickled out, just a spot at first but soon spreading onto the pillow after he had lain her down so gently. He had not meant it. He had not meant anything like it. He did not even remember what he had meant, and that was the truth. He had tried to tell her that, practically at the moment it had happened, but then it was too late. And it was too late now. It would always be too late.

He lowered his head.

When he opened his eyes again, he was looking at the paper.

At the top of the page, perfectly centered, was the title. It said:

YOU CAN GO NOW.

Dennis Etchison

TODAY'S SPECIAL

"How about some nice bottom round steak?" asked Avratin the butcher. "Is today's special."

"No round steak."

"Ah. Well, Mrs. Teola —"

"Taylor."

"— Mrs. Taylor." Avratin the butcher tapped the trays behind the open glass, then thumbed back another display of cuts. "I got some nice, nice clods, can cut for Swiss steak if —"

"No Swiss steak."

Avratin started to sigh, pinched off his nose with his thick curving forefinger, which was getting cold. "Excuse me. I know what you want. For you, some nice, nice, very nice pot —"

"No pot roast, neither."

His hands began describing in the air. "Some lovely chuck, some darling rump, a little —" He squeezed the air. "— Tender, juicy flank steak, eh?" He saw her turn away, the gray bun at the back of her neck beginning to wag. "Some brisket for boiling!" He heard his wife's heavy heels in the sawdust and at that slapped his forehead with both hands — *I give up* — for her to see.

"My, you're looking very well today," Avratin's wife cooed.

Muttering, Avratin slid the last tray back in place, grumbling to himself, sifting the red chunks of beef tenderloin through his fingers, which were now quite cold; the meat plopped back onto the paper liner and he slammed the glass, knocking the parsley loose from the top of the ground round.

"Yeah, you should hope you don't see my sister, Rose."

"Oh, Ro-sie. And how is her operation?"

"Don't ask."

"Well, Mrs. Teo —"

"Taylor. Taylor! My husband puts Teola in the book, nobody calls him." The gray bun wagged in growing impatience. "But now he's Manny Taylor. Manny Taylor! I want you tell me, would you call from the yellow pages a man with the name Manny Taylor?"

"Well," began Avratin's wife, standing closer to her husband, "what's good for your mister's business —"

"We should all live so long, I promise you. My God, my God." She shook her bun and hunched toward the door.

Avratin's wife cleared her throat. "Today special, we have some very nice fish, Mrs. Taylor," she called sweetly and waited for the woman to turn back under the creaking overhead fan.

"You got nothing I want," said the woman finally, only half-turning, shifting her brown carry-all to her other hand.

"Why, Mrs. Taylor," sang Avratin's wife. "You've been our faithful customer for thirteen years. Those years, they mean only that you should come to this? You're taking your business elsewhere now? God forbid that Lou and I should forget *our* friends so easy."

"You should talk, dearies. *You* should *talk!*" This she said directly to Avratin, sizing him up in his white apron as if he were an imposter. "You get Luttfisk back, then maybe we talk meat. That Luttfisk, he *knows* meat!" And she shuffled out the door.

A moment later, to no one in particular, to the passing cars, to the old man at the curb with the white beard and the stiff black hat, Avratin's wife called, "My Lou, he was owning this shop before that Luttfisk was starting in the business! Don't you forget that!"

But Avratin was shaking his head, reaching around to untie the strings, throwing his apron on the hook.

"Louie?"

He headed across the empty store to the back.

"Ask me why I'm closing an hour early. But ask me! Go ahead! You ask me about business, and I'll tell you. Business ... is ... lousy!"

Avratin's wife threw up her hands, imploring the ceiling fan to do something, anything.

In the tiny bedroom, by a single small lamp with the crisp, yellowed cellophane still clinging to the shade, with the sound turned down on the Johnny Carson Show, Avratin and his wife were having an argument.

"... Twenty years in the retail meat business and you knife me in the back. Twenty years putting bread on your plate, only to have you —"

"Listen to this! He's too proud, too proud to admit a mistake ..."

"— Twist, twisting the knife!"

Reproach, recrimination, guilt, counter-accusation, self-deprecation. The old pattern.

And only to come to this: that at the end, the finish, before grumbling into bed, during the sermonette, Avratin raised his hurt face to the water-stained ceiling one last time to declare, before the gods and whatever other audience might be listening:

"All right, I take care of it, I take care of everything. No matter that Luttfisk tries to rob me, his own partner. I get a man can take care of the job. I promise you, the problem be fixed, once-for-all!"

At the Century-Cudahy Storage and Packing Co., the White Collar Butcher was a very important man. No one at the plant could say exactly why, though it had to do with the fact that he was the best butcher in the county, that he had the finest set of tools anyone had ever laid eyes on, and the obvious quiet pride he took in his work. It had to do with the way he picked his own shifts, coming in unpredictably and always with the attitude of a man who has

The Dark Country   **99**

already been at work for several hours. It had to do with the air of authority he carried with him into the walk-in, the indefinable look of knowing something that he would never tell on his thin, expressionless lips, his smooth, ageless face, his small steel-blue eyes that were perpetually set on a place somewhere beyond the carcasses and the warehouse.

Alone at night, the White Collar Butcher stood motionless before the freezer, his eyes on the temperature gauge. But they were not focused there. Then, slowly, surely, he turned his back on the hook beam scales and stood over his meat block. He moved his hand from the evenly beveled edges to the guard at the right of the block. His hand was heavy, a special tool itself, quite perfectly balanced, smooth and pink and tapered ideally to the handles which he now allowed his fingers to play over lightly: the meat saw, the cleaver, the steak knife, the boning knife, below them the small scale, the aluminum trays, the spool of twine and, to the left, the blackboard. Then, with smooth, automatic, practiced moves he took down his tools one by one and washed them, wiped them and rubbed the handles, proceeded to sharpen them on the slow grinding wheel and then the whetstone, touched up the edges with the steel and wrapped them individually in soft, protective leather.

He set the pouches out neatly and then, by reflex acquired through years of practice, slipped his hand into his trouser pocket and withdrew a folded square of white paper. With one hand he opened it and read the name and address printed there with a grease pencil in straight block letters. *The name and address.*

He refolded it and slid it back into his pocket under the apron.

Another job.

Then, positioning in an easy, familiar stance, he reached for the wire brush and steel scraper and box of salt and began cleaning his cutting block, employing short, sure motions with his strong arms and shoulders, conserving his energy for the job to come. And as he worked on into the night, his tanned face and immaculately styled hair set off tastefully above the high, fashionable collar and wide hand-sewn tie that lay smoothly against his tailored shirt of imported silk, the whole effect suggesting a means far beyond his butcher's salary, was that perhaps the beginning of a narrow, bloodless smile that pinched the corners of his thin, efficient, professional lips?

For five nights Avratin hammered his pillow and spent more time than he should have in the cramped bathroom. Then the good news arrived.

Up went the noisy butcher paper painted with the proclamation he had kept rolled and hidden for three days now. He was nervous with anticipation as he tore off strips of masking tape and slapped it up across the plate glass windows. It covered the whole front of the store, right over the futile daily specials from the week past, as well it should have.

The first customers of the day were already waiting at the door when Avratin's wife finished dressing and joined her husband.

She stopped in the middle of the fresh sawdust floor, looking about as if by some transmogrification of sleep she had just walked into a strange, new life, or at least someone else's store. She smoothed her hair and gaped, turning around and around.

"This is a holiday? Or I'm sleeping still. Pinch me, Lou."

Avratin had pulled out all the trays in the meat case and was busy arranging his new, large display.

"Take it easy, take it easy, Rachel. You got your wish."

The last parking space in front filled up, and at last Avratin stood and leaned back and watched the women milling around on the sidewalk, pointing excitedly to the sign. He smiled a special smile that he had not used in years.

"Lou! Lou! Lou! You didn't do nothing too drastic, did you?" Then what he had said seemed to hit her.

She clipped to the door, shook the knob, apologized to the woman with the gray bun who was first in line, hurried back to get the keys, almost ran to the door and opened it.

Avratin watched her outside, shading her eyes, holding off their questions until she could get a good look at it herself.

She stood with one hand on her hip, one hand above her eyes, reading and rereading the banner with disbelief.

The women scrambled inside, heading for the meat case. He leaned back on his hands, watching them over the scales, a bright morning chill of anticipation tingling in his blood.

They stopped in front of the case, staring for long seconds.

Avratin wanted to speak to them, but held himself in check a moment longer.

His wife was the last to enter the store. She pushed her way through the inert bodies, ignoring the still, dulled faces on a few of which was beginning to dawn the first dim, uncomprehending light of recognition.

"Lou, I saw the sign," she beamed. "Is it true? Is it? Where is he?"

Avratin leaned forward. He spread his arms behind the transparent case in a gesture of supplication, palms out. His eyes rolled up to the creaking, slowly revolving fan and then returned to the display, newly arrived from the man in the high white collar, which he had just now finished arranging so carefully under the glass, the whole length of the counter, to the new cuts, strange cuts, so invitingly laid out, preserved by the cold, here something red, there something brown and almost recognizable, there a fine shank, there an opened ribcage, there a portion of a face you knew so well you almost expected it to greet you.

"Here," Avratin answered, in a voice he had not used in years. "Here! Can't you read the sign?

"LUTTFISK IS BACK!"

Very shortly thereafter the short, muffled cries began.

THE MACHINE DEMANDS
A SACRIFICE

Soot fell in a continuous haze that obliterated the sun over the freeway, leaving a gritty texture on the once-bright finishes of the variegated cars and trucks. For miles ahead they extended bumper to bumper in a snaking line, stretching on through infinite gradations of opaque smog, and if you let your arm hang down from the window and brushed the door with your fingertips, they would come away grainy and black-edged and imprinted with hundreds of microscopic lacerations.

It was five o'clock in Los Angeles on a July afternoon.

A short black van with the words E•MER•GEN•Z•INC stenciled on the sides was stalled in the far right lane.

"Jeezus," said the driver, wiping the sweat out of his eyes with a dirty sleeve. His face was bloated like a brown paper bag full of potatoes, his black eyes peering out through two torn, badly placed holes. "It's that fuel pump again — you know that, don't you?" He shook his head and glared outside for confirmation.

"I thought the Company was supposed to put in a rebuilt one, after last time," said the other, a slight young man named Jaime who was new on the job, with exaggerated disgust. This was in fact only the end of his first work week, and he still looked to the fat man for direction, trying to limit his end of the conversation to a general swearing, bitching echo.

"Jeezus H. Christ," said the fat man, hunching over the wheel and shifting his huge buttocks.

A horn started up behind them.

The fat man shook his head at the floorboard. "I *am* the Company, me and Raoul. *Told* that son of a bitch — but no, he's worried we'll miss some nice, juicy accident if I put 'er in the shop till noon. Man, I tell you ..."

"Yeah," said Jaime. "Well, hell, I'll get out and push the son of a bitch. There's a crashpad right up ahead. Thank God at least for that."

He climbed down from his side and went around to the back. The driver got out and pushed at the door, straining to reach the wheel inside. There was a wide shoulder by the side of the freeway, only yards ahead. After a few nauseous grunts through carbon monoxide and bleating horns, the driver hoisted himself in and braked as the van rolled to a stop in front of the compactor.

"Far enough," he gasped, stumbling out. "Don't want to junk this baby yet. God *damn.* Get too close and the junker takes over."

Jaime stood around trying to look grim, kicking rocks off the blacktop.

"Now we just got to wait for it to cool. How much credit we got on the card register, kid?"

"Uh, the starting fund from this morning, plus that two-car we found. The digits we sold 'em. Not much."

"Great. All we need's a COPter to spot us right now." The fat man leaned on the magnetic grapple of the compactor and let a sigh whistle out through his small mouth. "The junk fee on the van would just about pay the breakdown fine," he laughed bitterly. "They got it figured so it comes out *exactly* even, that's what I think."

"Yeah. Except for the vacutract unit," said Jaime. "Right, Jesse?"

But the fat man was looking back over his shoulder, past the massive compactor.

He stuck a thick finger to his lips. He motioned to the

kid, a rat-shrewd light coming into his eyes.

Jaime walked over, keeping behind the line of the automatic junking machine. He bobbed his head around the crane where Jesse indicated and saw it.

An '89 sedan with a selenium top was racked up at close to a 45 degree angle, the right side crumpled against the pavement from hood to tail. A man in a business suit with spider webs of blood spun from his ear and forehead was laid out on the front seat. A thin man with glasses was reaching up and in the opened driver's door, tending the wounds.

"Watch this," mouthed Jesse, trying to force his shirttails back into his belt under the light smock.

He stepped boldly around the compactor. "What happened here? He hit the rail?"

The man with glasses half-turned, startled. He quickly sized up Jesse and his partner — too quickly, thought Jaime, his heart dropping.

"I'm a doctor," announced the man. He started toward his own car, parked at the end of the pad. Just then the bottleneck ahead on the freeway unclogged momentarily, for the river of stagnating cars revved up and surged forward a few choppy feet. "Just — let this be," sighed the doctor arbitrarily, flattening his hands in the haze. "I've got him sedated right now."

Jesse ambled forward. "Looks like you're pretty near to having a dead man on your hands, doc," he said.

"Who are you people?" snapped the doctor.

"We were just passing by. Our unit's back there. Thought we might be of some —"

The doctor's cool gray eyes flicked between the two men. "You thought you might make a bootleg sale or two, eh? Well, you can just go on. Go on, now."

"We're in business to help people, same as you, sir. Now if this is an emergency, why, you know, we might be in a position to help you save this poor guy's life." Jesse stepped closer. "Any internal injuries?"

"Listen, you. I'm the doctor. I pulled off to assist, and I can only hope to God I'm not too late. I've already called for an ambulance. This man is going to Central Receiving. Go on now, get going, before I call for a COPter."

"Uh, your ambulance is close by, is it?"

The doctor fumbled with his stethoscope and shook it at Jesse. It flopped like a serpent. Impatient and indignant, he strode up to Jesse and almost struck him across the face with it.

Jaime looked down at his fingernails.

"Under the laws of the State of California I can have you arrested," threatened the doctor. "You realize that?"

"Don't know what you're getting at," said Jesse cordially. "Mr. Sandoval here and I were just returning from a two-car call on the Ventura Freeway and —"

"Not only your license to buy and sell," continued the doctor, "but my own license to practice. Oh, I know your game, all right. I know how you independents operate. I wasn't born yesterday. Moving in like vultures when you spot a quick touch, taking what you want with or without authorization, selling your wares to anyone fool or desperate enough not to ask questions! I'm going to call in a complaint right now." He turned and headed for the red phone box on the rail. *What's the number on your van?*"

Jaime, facing backwards, touched his partner's arm. "Hey, Jesse, maybe we better ..."

Just then an undulating wail, unnoticed till now, increased to an ear-splitting level and an ambulance, long and shiny with Day-Glow lights flashing, screeched up the connecting ramp. Its doors and tailgate flung open and a stretcher touched down before it had stopped. Two antiseptic attendants sprang down and snapped back a side panel. A new portable vacutrans unit gleamed at the ready. They lugged it out and headed for the wreck.

Jaime looked at Jesse.

"Jeezus H. Christ," said Jesse. "Looks like the sons of bitches beat us out again." He ran his stubby fingers through his short, oily black hair. "Come on, kid," he muttered. "Let's get out of here. We're wasting time."

"Do you think the van'll start now?"

Jesse whistled two descending notes. "Get in," he said.

Jaime got in. He ground the starter again and again.

"Come on, come on," growled Jesse. He climbed in and struggled with the engine cover between the seats. "I think I hear something. Let's go. Piss on it. God damn, I'll get it going."

He yanked his smock up under his arms. His shirt was unbuttoned halfway already. Jaime saw the wide segmented plastic belt hanging over Jesse's belly and swallowed his surprise, He watched Jesse unhook the belt, position it above the overheated fuel pump and pull the stopper. Amber liquid poured down over the metal, steaming, until the reservoir was empty. Jaime stuck his head out the window and took a breath.

A whirring sound began in his ear. He moved his hand to brush it away. Then he noticed the COPter dipping low. The policeman touched down on the other side of the compactor.

"Hey," suggested Jaime.

"Don't tell me."

The policeman lowered his arm, stopped the whirling blades and folded them back into the nightstick. He went to the wrecked vehicle first.

"That'll cool her down," grunted Jesse, fastening the empty belt and covering it again with his clothing.

Jaime floored the accelerator and twisted the key. The engine turned over and caught.

"Tromp on it," said Jesse.

They cut away from the freeway, slipped back onto the Harbor at Eighth and connected with the Santa Monica, The traffic smoothed out a little. They passed an empty Chinese GT buckied against the Adams off, an overturned milk tanker covered with flies in the center lane at La Brea, an impossible-looking two-car head-on at the Robertson on-ramp, five or six stalled cars on or near the next few crashpads at quarter-mile intervals and a grotesque four-car pileup smeared across as many lanes just before Washington. Jaime slowed, but Jesse pointed at the two independent units already converging on the scene; it wasn't worth their time. Above it all, lacing the sky in a dense crosshatching, were the circling COPters, officers of the law hand-strapped to their spinning, humming nightsticks, about to drop in a black swarm.

"I thought he was gonna stop us back there."

"What? Aw, they know their job. They can't hassle a unit doing legal business at an accident."

"Good thing we got started, anyway," said Jaime. "The fine for a breakdown on —".

"The bastards."

The van roared on.

"I think it's about six, Jesse."

"Don't rub it in. But we can't go back yet. I got a wife and kid to feed."

"I guess I'm lucky," said Jaime.

"My kid, she ain't got a tooth in her head. My wife made one big mistake, that's for sure."

They passed the LAST SANTA MONICA EXIT sign.

"She loses a tooth, my wife tells her to put it under her pillow for the fairy. Some fairy. I leave her a quarter. Next thing you know, she's pullin' out teeth to get more money. I can't afford to give her no allowance. She's a good kid, real smart, she understands — business is tough. But this fairy shit. I don't have the heart to tell her. So pretty soon she's got no more teeth. Whadaya think of that? Take this street here."

They prowled the blocks off Lincoln, Jesse calling the turns, and found themselves eventually on Navy. Jesse dipped his head, scanning the small houses and narrow corners in the protracted twilight.

"This is more like it," he said.

They hung a left and steered on deeper into a disintegrating neighborhood. Jaime felt tense. Once they passed an automatic patrol; Jaime straightened his arm to wave, caught himself when he heard Jesse snicker, and pretended to adjust the sideview mirror instead. He had to remind himself that nothing more than a TV scanner swept the passing streets from behind the aluminized windows.

Jaime felt a familiar fear throbbing low in his back.

"Turn here," ordered Jesse. The tips of his fingers rubbed together.

"Here?"

"Yeah. I can feel it. Can't you?"

Jaime started to shrug, stopped. "I'm ... not sure," he said.

Halfway along the short block, parked at an odd angle, was an old sedan. Years of unrepaired dents trimmed the body, a few half-heartedly pounded out and coated with fading primer, the edges of the dents now rusted in permanently. A shadow moved to one side within the car and a dark shape shifted by the open passenger door.

"Well well," said Jesse, "let's see what we got here."

The van cut its lights, passed slowly.

"We got one," announced Jesse.

They pulled up in front of the car.

Jesse studied the rearview mirror. "All right, boy," he said. "Let me do the talking." He jerked open his door and lumbered to the curb.

"Hello, good evening. Any trouble here?"

A woman stood up uncertainly. Jaime saw her; something stirred in him. "Why, uh, ye-es," she said, eyeing them, their van. Then, relieved into a decision: "Can you help me, please?"

Jesse grew bolder. "Let's just see what the trouble is here." He spoke with authority. "Stand aside," he ordered.

Jaime edged out and watched by the van. His senior partner certainly knew his job — there was no doubt about that now — and he tried to listen to catch a few pointers.

"... Just went out of control," she was saying. It was hard to hear. Two little faces studied Jaime from the window. She went on explaining how her husband had lost control of the car. "Just keeled over" were the words she used over and over.

"Get the litter," yelled Jesse.

The young man swung open the back panel and brought the water litter, flipping on the heater in the handle. An overweight man in a metallic green suit was

The Dark Country   **109**

sprawled on the front seat. They turned his legs and Jesse cradled his head, not too carefully, thought Jaime, as they hauled him out. His hat with the fishing lure in the band fell into the gutter.

"You going to be all right," the woman said over the man. "Oooh ..."

They wheeled the litter to the van. The water pad slogged and gurgled under the body. Jesse pulled a lever and the tailgate lifted them inside.

Jesse strapped an electrode plate over the chest. He clicked on the diagnostic scanner and checked the dials hurriedly, preoccupied. The man groaned and the respiration dial wavered.

"He all right? Isn't he?" the woman called in a high voice from outside.

Jesse shot a look at the young man. It pressed him hard, relentlessly, and Jaime felt himself shrinking in his clothes.

With a grunt Jesse stumbled out and walked ominously to the car. He clasped his hands at his back and lowered his head.

Jaime heard him say, "Your husband — he is your husband, right?"

"Yes sir, we just ..."

"Well, your husband is dead. At the present time."

She protested, then raged, then wailed, but Jesse talked her through it. At last she nearly collapsed against the car. Jaime had seen it before. Only this time the sequence wasn't right. He was confused.

"Well, do something, please! Oh sweet Lord!"

"I think we caught him in time," said Jesse. "But if we had put him in suspension just a few minutes earlier —"

"Oh, Lord, Lord ...!"

"I can try, that's all I can do. Uh, I'll need your card."

The woman opened the car door and practically fell inside. One of the children started crying. She dumped out her handbag and clawed through the contents.

Jesse took the credit plate from her. "We'll be right with you, he said. "I wish I could make you a firm promise. But we'll do our best," he added, almost cheerfully.

Back in the van, Jesse snapped his fingers. "Run a thermal on him," he barked.

"Jesse, why did you say he was dead?"

"Talk later! Get on the stick! We don't want no interference to drive up."

Jaime turned on the thermal table and watched the scope nervously as the shapes of organs wavered into bright color focus on the analyzer. The lungs expanded, shrank, the heart hesitated, swelled, pulsed feebly. Most of the colors were right. But streaming heat outlines of the wrong color clotted the pulmonary artery. The victim, his body a rising, straining knot, labored through congested membranes for breath.

Jesse took out a syringe.

"Give him this, quick. I don't want him to check out ahead of time. Or we'll have to work mighty fast. He isn't even in suspension. It's a massive coronary, looks like." He riffled the plastic overleaves of the anatomy directory, found the page. "Yeah. What's it matter? He's gone anyway."

"What won't matter, Jesse?" asked the young man, slipping the needle under a pinch of ashen skin.

"You're about to learn a lesson, boy. A big one."

He bounced around the interior of the van, flicking on the vacutract unit, turning on the UV in the body dome overhead, checking the temperature on the storage compartment, cursing when he snagged his jagged thumbnail on his smock. He switched on the autoclave and dared it to heat fast enough.

He hovered, his belly hanging over the edge of the table. "No dice. Adrenalin's not enough, eh? Good, fine, I don't care."

"Jesse?"

"*Wha-at.* Get his clothes off."

Jaime wanted to ask what they were doing. How they could operate without a certificate of death from a doctor or a requisition for parts from a regular ambulance unit. Wanted to know if Jesse was worried about their license to extract and sell. Wanted to know why — but he understood why Jesse had said the man was dead already now as the plastic blimp descended from the roof and suctioned onto the body like a leech. It was too late, anyway. The laser knife made its first incision.

"Sure, Jesse. I got it."

The autowaldoes whispered in unison, almost with anticipation under the bubble. At the first stroke came a cry from outside the van as the wife fell in despair. At the same instant a bubbling groan came from the man on the table. Then the last breath whistled out of him like air from a shriveling balloon. Jesse punched a pattern for kidneys, spleen, gall bladder, pancreas, for nearly everthing but the overtasked heart. And the liver. "Damn liver," he mumbled disgustedly. "He was a boozer, the lousy —" The stainless steel pincers poised and peeled back layers and lifted and groped, severed and sutured and weighed, calipered and deposited the organs in the vacuum tube to the nitrogen bank and then finished up neatly with a muffled sucking sound. The scissor-point fingers suspended over the corpse, flashing and switching for a moment, and then retracted. The body was left gutted.

Jamie tried to say something.

"Don't mean a thing, kid. He's garbage now."

Jamie heard the sound of a car passing far away, a bird on the wires outside, the racing of his own heart. He didn't know anything to say.

His partner pulled a body envelope out of the 'clave, wrapped the body, sealed it with the sealing iron. Seconds, minutes passed but Jaime could think of nothing to say.

He saw Jesse wheel the litter to the tailgate, press the button to lower it, climb out and push it to the old car. The woman screamed. She seemed to lose her mind when she saw it. Jesse struggled with her until he could inject her with a tranquilizer. She slumped into the car. He tossed the credit plate in after her. Then he put the bag by the lamppost on the cracked sidewalk. The bulb was burned out but Jaime saw clearly the formless encapsulated remains like a giant slug caught on the cement. He saw the two little black faces staring and crying. The children were jumping up and down on the car seat now. They kept their fingers in their mouths; spittle ran down their dark wrists, leaving their cold fingers glistening. Tears streamed alongside their flat noses, shining them, and their brown eyes wavered and glittered like jewels. When Jesse started toward them with needles Jaime called out. Tried to call out. His throat was a single dry, painful muscle. He bit down until his jaws hurt. Their eyes were looking at him.

Jesse headed back to the van.

"Get out! Up front! We're not clear yet."

Jaime moved but not fast enough. Jesse grabbed him by the smock and flung him toward the cab. "Start it up. Start it!"

Jesse took over. He stuffed Jaime into the front seat and gunned the engine. His ferret eyes darted about the empty street. "We got to make this look right." He slammed into reverse, drew back, shifted into first and pulled up to the tail of the car. Then he locked against the car and rammed it forward into the lamppost. There was a grinding and a buckling of metal and a splintering of glass. A piece of the lamp hit the top of the car, rolled off and shattered on the street into a million unrepairable fragments.

On the way back, Jesse would not stop talking.

"That coon'll never find out who we were," he was saying. "Just like we used to do it in 'Nam. The first 'tract and 'trans units came in while I was over there. We used to keep the ARVN forces up with transes from the body count. 'Got to keep the war machine running!' they told us. Then there wasn't enough. We finally had to get into our own casualties. The NCOs told us to get what we needed off our own. They wouldn't let us take nothing off the whites. We got some of the brown brothers together and made sure ours got left alone. We had to look somewhere. Most of the civilians, the gooks, were too small. Women, kids. So we came down on the nigger bodies. We made *sure* there were always enough of 'em. Then they started 'transing state-side. Right away there were too many patients, not enough donors. I coulda told 'em *that* was gonna happen. So when we got on the outs we went into business, me and Raoul. We wasn't the only ones. There are plenty of units like us. Sure, plenty now."

Jesse settled back, moving his belly behind the wheel. "Whatsamatter, kid? We made a good hit." He patted the thermostat. "We'll sell 'em tomorrow, Or the next day. Don't worry."

They squealed around a corner and headed up the long gray ramp to the freeway. They passed a collison but two independent units were wheeled into place next to it already, the two drivers haggling over the rights. Jaime saw a fist pounding the air.

"Me, now I got something to worry about." Jesse yanked the drainage belt loose under his smock. "Damn pisser. Gotta get me some new kidneys. You ever have a tube runnin' up your dick? I'll get 'em, though. That's for sure. Long as it's not off no damn spade."

They sped past accident after accident, metal and chrome and flesh spattered over and over again across lanes for miles, as if part of the same accident. And always the vans moving in from all directions, cutting across dividers, heading against the traffic, closing in.

"I need a lotta stuff, just for myself." Jesse bit fiercely at his torn thumbnail. "Old ticker won't hold up forever. Not to mention the rest of me. Get pains in the middle of the night, you know?"

He turned his head on the thick stalk of his neck.

He glanced across at Jaime. His eyes roamed over Jaime's thin body, the strong young muscles, the firm abdomen. He smiled, a crack splitting his cruel brown face.

Jaime was hypnotized by the passing lights. His eyes focused on the sideview mirror outside the door. He saw that his jaw hung slack, his mouth half open as if to speak, as it had been for mile after endless mile. He saw the white, sharp, strong teeth, good teeth, the kind anyone would be proud to own. He sat gripping the religious medal around

114

his neck, so tightly it burned his hand.

"Don't let it get to you, kid. It's that damn smog. It's worse'n a sacka onions." He slid his fleshy hands down to the bottom of the steering wheel. "But it's all in a day's work, I guess. Be home with my wife an' kid in a few more mintues. Welcome to the Company, Jaime. We *need* somebody like you. Believe me." When he heard no answer he said, "That is your name, right? Jaime?"

But Jaime did not hear him. He was back on the dark street, waiting, but she would not stop. She would not stop screaming.

Dennis Etchison

CALLING ALL MONSTERS

The first thing I see is the white light.

And I think: so they have taken me to one of those places. I knew it. That was why the pain. My brain stops spinning like a cracked gyroscope long enough for me to relax. Then I get it, all of it. And I think I may go mad, if it is true.

A rubber hand closes my eyes and I see red again. Black lightning forks shimmer in a kind of bas-relief in front of me. Then the whirling stains settle in. I think they are Rorschach tests. The black shapes flow like ink on a blotter. I look into the first one. It seems to me to be an accident. I see a car, no, two cars, and the smaller one is jackknifed over the big one. Then the pain starts again at the back of my head, not throbbing like before but only dull and steady like a hot light bulb so I try not to think any more about the ink blot.

The voices again over me. They drone, too slow, hurting my ears, trying to seep in through the hardening blockages I can feel there, especially the low one that sounds like the man has a greasy tongue. I want them to stop but they continue, the greasy tongue bending closer. Then I understand, but don't understand, because I know he must be speaking a foreign language. I want the sound to stop. They always speak in foreign languages or at least thick, oleaginous accents, slow and heavy until they give the orders, then harsh and guttural. I remember. I want it to stop because it hurts me. Don't they care? It hurts me!

"I'm sorry" says the man, slipping his hands into his coat pockets. "But it's too late for us to do anything."

But of course it hurts me. That is part of it. I remember now. It is always that way. They even called it the House of Pain once, didn't they? Yes, and the accent oppressive and stressed where you didn't expect it to be and he never bothered about anesthesia. I believe he said it was a shortage of supplies on the island but I don't believe that. I think for him it was a House of Pleasure.

Yes, that is what they are doing. That is what they are doing. Maybe I keep forgetting, keep drifting off because it is less painful that way. My heart doesn't speed when I think of it. You would think it would. All I feel there is the hardness, cold and brassy and clammy, over my heart. I don't understand that part yet but somehow it seems to fit.

I am bound. I know that now. The cool pressure around my rib cage loosens like a mummy's fingers and the cold lifts from my heart, leaving a sticky spot there. I strain mightily to move my arms and legs but still they won't work. Strapped. I get it more clearly. Lifting, there was lifting right after the start of the pain, and even then I couldn't move, so I must have been bound even then, and more lifting, always higher. But I played it smart. I kept my eyes closed. I knew what was coming. I didn't need my eyes to tell me where they were taking me. It was up lots of stairs, almost always, the top of an old building, tons of sweating stone blocks crumbling in the mortar and piles of dust and powdered limestone in corners where the torches never reached, and the stairs wound in a spiral up and down, down to the dungeons but they took me up, up to the laboratory. They always take them up at first. To the skylight. But now it must be night, the light artificial. They always worked at night on the important experiments.

"I'm sorry "says the man in charge, hiding his powdered hands in his white coat. "But it's too late for us to do anything to save him. We've run all the standard tests, and so now ..."
He makes a helpless gesture.

Something smooth and lightly textured brushes my chin, my lips, my nose, my brow. Now the red darkens. I hear the swish of starched smocks. There are several of them. They move surely, impatiently. So this is a big one. Not just the ubiquitous assistant but others, experts from all over have come to observe. The low voices grind again, like old automobiles on cold mornings with the electrolyte low.

They hurry, I feel it in my skin more than hear it. It must be night. The air they stir toward me is cold. I grow colder. Even my head. Funny but as the cold spreads up from my neck the spot at the back of my head aches less and less. That is, I suppose, some kind of relief.

But still I am afraid.

I wait for the generators to start up. They always need them for electricity. I hear no lightning. So they must use the generators to rev up their particle chambers, their glowing vacuum tubes, their bubbling flasks of colored fluids, their magnetic arcs jumping and sweeping up and up and up the conductor rods. Snapping and crackling, humming and spinning rotors that whir and whine and buzz. I used to like them. I think of the lightning bugs I used to collect in mayonnaise jars. They sparked and jumped on the sill all night and it reminded me of their experiments, and the thought scared me a little but it was still pleasurable, a sublimely creepy game I played on myself that always slipped me off into a comfortable dream.

The difference now is that I can't wake up.

I hear a hum. They are ready.

"I'm sorry," says the man in charge, hiding his powdered hands in a wrinkled white coat. "But it's too late for us to do anything to save your husband. We've run all the standard tests, and so now ..." He bares his hands nervously and moves them in a helpless gesture.

The woman bursts into tears. "But you can't! I showed you the will, notarized, carried with me all these years! And the copy in his pocket!"

The doctor fumbles through his papers. "I can show you

his EKG. Here, see for yourself"

As the machinery is lowered over me on damped hinges, I can no longer feel the pain in my head. Sounds, sensations are receding. I wonder if it is the head they are after. I remember such a head, floating in a porcelain tray, clear tubes of nutrient running in through the nostrils, stained bandages pinned around the crown. The eyes were open, and so maybe it will not be so bad. And the head went on thinking. What did it think? Let me try— yes, the door, the one with the heavy bar in front. And the sliding window at the base for food. Another experiment. The head, released from physical demands, focused its powers to make contact and control. Even the deformed monster from the previous operation. He controlled the creature behind the door, calling it out to smash through the boards a —

But now they fit it over my abdomen. I can no longer feel there but I know that is where the instrument is clamping down. That is where they always start.

I wonder if my table is mounted to swivel, to turn me upright. I hear the sheet rustling down below. They may, since I am strapped so completely I can't move a toe or finger. I hear the clasping of surgical steel. It begins.

"I'm sorry," says the doctor in charge, quickly hiding his pale-powdered hands deep in his wrinkled, blood-smeared white coat. "But it's too late for us to do anything to save your husband. We've run the standard tests for death and there is just no response, nothing. I am sorry. So now..." He bares his shriveled hands furtively and moves them in a helpless gesture of absolution.

The wife erupts in tears of frustration and rage. "But you can't operate yet! I showed you the will, notarized, carried with me all these years, since the first time. And the copy of the instructions in his wallet, and the neck chain, you found them at the accident tonight! What more does it take?"

The doctor ducks her freezing gaze and agitates his papers, moistening a finger. "Let me show you his EKG. Here,

120

*you can see for yourself, no activity whatever. I'm sorry, but
we have to go ahead, do you see? We can't afford to risk any
further deterioration. We have the other clause to consider,
the main clause."*

For the love of God I can't feel but I can hear it slicing
away. Why can't I feel? They must use anesthetic now but
even so I know what fiends they are. I think I always knew.
O now the obscene sucking sound growing fainter even as
my hearing dissolves, wet tissue pulling apart. They suction
my bood, the incision clamped wide like another mouth a
monstrous Caesarean and I hear the shiny scissors clipping
tissues clipping fat, the automated scalpels striking tictac-
toe on my torso and I know they are taking me, the blood
in my head tingles draining down down and I am almost
gone, O what is it what are they doing to me the monsters
ME they must be it can't be that other nono my papers
they couldn't do THAT they couldn't break the terms it says
in blackandwhite NO so it has to be like those other times I
have seen the altered specimen on the table the wrapped
composite the sutured One Who Waits drifting in fluid for
the new brain the shaved skin the transplanted claws the
feral rictus the excised hump promised long ago the suddenly stripped subcutaneous map scarred creations I call
you in

"The main clause."
*"B-but that was conditional, you can read —!" She comes
close to blowing it then, nearly falling all over herself in a
quivering puddle right there in the hospital corrido, She tries
one last time. "He — he wanted the contract, a kind of extra
life insurance benefit for the children. But it meant more, a lot
more to him. It was really the last chance for him to do something for others, for humanity. But he got to be obsessed with
the technical question of dying, don't you understand? the
exact moment of death. When? He was never sure. When is it?
Can you prove it to me?"*
*"My dear lady, the heartbeat and respiration cease, the
muscles go slack ..."*

"God damn it, you cold fish! He wanted an EEG!"

The doctor backs off, assuming a professional stance. "Your husband agreed to sell his usable internal organs to the transplant bank for the usual fee which you, as his beneficiary, will receive within 60 days. Neither you nor your husband made any move to break the contract prior to his, eh, demise this evening and so, I'm afraid ... there is nothing further I am empowered to do. The standard tests of death have been administered in accordance with the laws of the state, and now his internal physical remains belong to the Nieborn Clinic. His personal effects, of course, remain yours — I'm sure they are at the front desk by now — as well as his, eh, other remains, which will be available to you for burial or cremation. In the morning. And now, if you'll excuse me, Mrs. ..."

She sobs. There is nothing else for her.

I call you now as always before you must return taste sweet revenge on these the true monsters break in now the floodgate opens the dam breaks the skylight shatters under deathlocked weight the torch is dropped the windmill collapses the trapdoor opens the tank splits and gushes controls are shortcircuited the surrogate returns the animal people cry ARE WE NOT MEN? at last the grafts rebel appendages reborn to murder I call you back I call you in now do not wait come as always to the laboratory House of Pain operating room crypt castle tower NOW I call you where are you? now I call you I call you I call you ARE WE NOT MEN? O God what forgotten corner have I walled myself into what have I done FOR THE LOVE OF GOD

The vacutract unit is shut off. The organs are sealed and deposited in liquid nitrogen. The heavy insulated door is closed, and the chrome catch padlocked. Rubber gloves are stripped. Leave the remains for the orderlies. It goes to the morgue anyway. But for God's sake keep that sheet over the face, so curiously distorted at the end.

The operation is a success.

the last thing I see is the blackness

THE DEAD LINE

This morning I put ground glass in my wife's eyes. She didn't mind. She didn't make a sound. She never does.

I took an empty bottle from the table. I wrapped it in a towel and swung it, smashing it gently against the side of her bed. When the glass shattered it made a faint, very faint sound like wind chimes in a thick fog. No one noticed, of course, least of all Karen. Then I placed it under my shoe and stepped down hard, rocking my weight back and forth until I felt fine sand underfoot. I knelt and picked up a few sharp grains on the end of my finger, rose and dropped them onto her corneas. First one, then the other. She doesn't blink, you know. It was easy.

Then I had to leave. I saw the technicians coming. But already it was too late; the damage had been done. I don't know if they found the mess under the bed. I suppose someone will. The janitors or the orderlies, perhaps. But it won't matter to them, I'm sure.

I slipped outside the glass observation wall as the technicians descended the lines, adjusting respirators, reading printouts and making notations on their pocket recorders. I remember that I thought then of clean, college-trained farmers combing rows of crops, checking the condition of the coming harvest, turning down a cover here, patting a loose mound there, touching the beds with a horticulturist's fussiness, ready to prune wherever necessary for the demands of the marketplace. They may not have seen me at all. And what if they had? What was I but a concerned husband come to pay his respects to a loved one? I might have been lectured about the risk of bringing unwanted germs into the area, though they must know how unlikely that is with the high-intensity UV lights and sonic purifiers and other sanitary precautions. I did make a point of passing near the Children's Communicable Diseases Ward on my way there, however; one always hopes.

Then, standing alone behind the windows, isolated and empty as an expectant father waiting for his flesh and blood to be delivered at last into his own hands, I had the sudden, unshakable feeling that I was being watched.

By whom?

The technicians were still intent on their readouts.

Another visitor? It was unlikely; hardly anyone else bothers to observe. A guilty few still do stop by during the lonely hours, seeking silent expiation from a friend, relative or lover, or merely to satisfy some morbid curiosity; the most recently-acquired neomorts usually receive dutiful visitations at the beginning, but invariably the newly-grieved are so overwhelmed by the impersonalness of the procedure that they soon learn to stay away to preserve their own sanity.

I kept careful track of the progress of the white coats on the other side of the windows, ready to move on at the first sign of undue concern over my wife's bed.

And it was then that I saw her face shining behind my own in the pane. She was alert and standing for the first time since the stroke, nearly eighteen months ago. I gripped the handrail until my nails were white, staring in disbelief at Karen's transparent reflection.

I turned. And shrank back against the wall. The cold sweat must have been on my face, because she reached out shakily and pressed my hand.

"Can I get you anything?"

Her hair was beautiful again, not the stringy, matted mass I had come to know. Her makeup was freshly applied, her lips dark at the edges and parted just so, opening on a warm, pink interior, her teeth no longer discolored but once more a luminous bone-white. And her eyes. They were perfect.

I lunged for her.

She sidestepped gracefully and supported my arm. I looked closely at her face as I allowed her to hold me a moment longer. There was nothing wrong with that, was there?

"Are you all right?" she said.

She was so much like Karen I had to stop the backs of my fingers from stroking the soft, wispy down at her temple, as they had done so many, many times. She had always liked that. And so, I remembered, had I; it was so long ago I had almost forgotten.

"Sorry," I managed. I adjusted my clothing, smoothing my hair down from the laminar airflow around the beds. "I'm not feeling well."

"I understand."

Did she?

"My name is Emily Richterhausen," she said.

I straightened and introduced myself. If she had seen me inside the restricted area she said nothing. But she couldn't have been here that long. I would have noticed her.

"A relative?" she asked.

"My wife."

"Has ... has she been here long?"

"Yes. I'm sorry. If you'll excuse me —"

"Are you sure you're all right?" She moved in front of me. "I could get you a cup of coffee, you know, from the machines. We could both have one. Or some water."

It was obvious that she wanted to talk. She needed it. Perhaps I did, too. I realized that I needed to explain myself, to pass off my presence before she could guess my plan.

"Do you come here often, Emily?" It was a foolish question. I knew I hadn't seen her before.

"It's my husband," she said.

"I see."

"Oh, he's not one of ... them. Not yet. He's in Intensive Care." The lovely face began to change. "A coma. It's been weeks. They say he may regain consciousness. One of the doctors said that. How long can it go on, do you know?"

I walked with her to a bench in the waiting area.

"An accident?" I said.

"A heart attack. He was driving to work. The car crossed the divider. It was awful." She fumbled for a handkerchief. I gave her mine. "They say it was a miracle he survived at all. You should have seen the car. No, you shouldn't have. No one should have. A miracle."

"Well," I told her, trying to sound comforting, "as I understand it, there is no 'usual' in comatose cases. It can go on indefinitely, as long as brain death hasn't occured. Until then there's always hope. I saw a news item the other day about a young man who woke up after four years. He asked if he had missed his homework assignment. You've probably heard —"

"Brain death," she repeated, mouthing the words uneasily. I saw her shudder.

"That's the latest Supreme Court ruling. Even then," I went on quickly, "there's still hope. You remember that girl in New Jersey? She's still alive. She may pull out of it at any time," I lied. "And there are others like her. A great many, in fact. Why —"

"There *is* hope, isn't there?"

"I'm sure of it," I said, as kindly as possible.

"But then," she said, "supposing ... What is it that actually happens, afterwards? How does it work? Oh, I know about the Maintenance and Cultivation Act. The doctor explained everything at the beginning, just in case." She glanced back toward the Neomort Ward and took a deep, uncertain breath. She didn't really want to know, not now. "It looks so nice and clean, doesn't it? They can still be of great service to society. The kidneys, the eyes, even the heart. It's a wonderful thing. Isn't it?"

"It's remarkable," I agreed. "Your husband, had he signed the papers?"

"No. He kept putting it off. William never liked to dwell on such matters. He didn't believe in courting disaster. Now I only wish I had forced him to talk about it, while there was still time."

"I'm sure it won't come to that," I said immediately. I couldn't bear the sight of her crying. "You'll see. The odds are very much on your side."

We sat side by side in silence as an orderly wheeled a stainless-steel cleaning cart off the elevator and headed past us to the observation area. I could not help but notice the special scent of her skin. Spring flowers. It was so unlike the hospital, the antisepticized cloud that hangs over everything until it has settled into the very pores of the skin. I studied her discreetly: the tiny, exquisite whorls of her ear, the blood pulsing rapidly and naturally beneath her healthy skin. Somewhere an electronic air ionizer was whirring, and a muffled bell began to chime in a distant hallway.

"Forgive me," she said. "I shouldn't have gone on like that. But tell me about your wife." She faced me. "Isn't it strange?" We were inches apart. "It's so reassuring to talk to someone else who understands. I don't think the doctors really know how it is for us, for those who wait."

"They can't," I said.

"I'm a good listener, really I am. William always said that."

"My — my wife signed the Universal Donor Release two years ago," I began reluctantly, "the last time she renewed her driver's license." Good until her next birthday, I thought. As simple as that. Too simple. Karen, how could you have known? How could I? I should have. I should have found out. I should have stopped your hand. "She's here now. She's been here since last year. Her electroencephalogram was certified almost immediately."

"It must be a comfort to you," she said, "to know that she didn't suffer."

"Yes."

"You know, this is the first time I've been on this particular floor. What is it they call it?" She was rattling on, perhaps to distract herself.

"The Bioemporium."

"Yes, that's it. I guess I wanted to see what it would be like, just in case. For my William." She tried bravely to smile. "Do you visit her often?"

"As often as possible."

"I'm sure that must mean a great deal."

To whom? I thought, but let it pass.

"Don't worry," I said. "Your husband will recover. He'll be fine. You'll see."

Our legs were touching. It had been so long since I had felt contact with sentient flesh. I thought of asking her for that cup of coffee now, or something more, in the cafeteria. Or a drink.

"I try to believe that," she said. "It's the only thing that keeps me going. None of this seems real, does it?"

She forced the delicate corners of her mouth up into a full smile.

"I really should be going now. I could get something for him, couldn't I? You know, in the gift shop downstairs? I'm told they have a very lovely store right here in the building. And then I'll be able to give it to him during visiting hours. When he wakes up."

"That's a good idea," I said.

She said decisively, "I don't think I'll be coming to this floor again."

"Good luck," I told her. "But first, if you'd like, Emily, I thought —"

"What was ... what is your wife's name? If you don't mind my asking?"

"Karen," I said. Karen. What was I thinking? Can you forgive me? You can do that, can't you, sweetheart?

"That's such a pretty name," she said.

"Thank you."

She stood. I did not try to delay her. There are some things that must be set to rest first, before one can go on. You helped remind me of that, didn't you, Karen? I nearly forgot. But you wouldn't let me.

"I suppose we won't be running into each other

again," she said. Her eyes were almost cheerful.

"No."

"Would you ... could you do me one small favor?"

I looked at her.

"What do you think I should get him? He has so many nice things. But you're a man. What would you like to have, if you were in the hospital? God forbid," she added, smiling warmly.

I sat there. I couldn't speak. I should have told her the truth then. But I couldn't. It would have seemed cruel, and that is not part of my nature.

What do you get, I wondered, for a man who has nothing?

2.

I awaken.

The phone is silent.

I go to the medicine cabinet, swallow another fistful of L-tryptophan tablets and settle back down restlessly, hoping for a long and mercifully dreamless nap.

Soon, all too soon and not soon enough, I fall into a deep and troubled sleep.

I awaken to find myself trapped in an airtight box.

I pound on the lid, kicking until my toes are broken and my elbows are torn and bleeding. I reach into my pocket for my lighter, an antique Zippo, thumb the flint. In the sudden flare I am able to read an engraved plate set into the satin. TWENTY-FIVE YEAR GUARANTEE, it says in fancy script. I scream. My throat tears. The lighter catches the white folds and tongues of flame lick my face, spreading rapidly down my squirming body. I inhale fire.

The lid swings open.

Two attendants in white are bending over me, squirting out the flames with a water hose. One of them chuckles.

Wonder how that happened? he says.

Spontaneous combustion? says his partner.

That would make our job a hell of a lot easier, says the

other. He coils the hose and I see through burned-away eyelids that it is attached to a sink at the head of a stainless-steel table. The table has grooves running along the sides and a drainage hole at one end.

I scream again, but no sound comes out.

They turn away.

I struggle up out of the coffin. There is no pain. How can that be? I claw at my clothing, baring my seared flesh.

See? I cry. I'm alive!

They do not hear.

I rip at my chest with smoldering hands, the peeled skin rolling up under my fingernails. See the blood in my veins? I shout. I'm not one of them!

Do we have to do this one over? asks the attendant. It's only a cremation. Who'll know?

I see the eviscerated remains of others glistening in the sink, in the jars and plastic bags. I grab a scalpel. I slash at my arm. I cut through the smoking cloth of my shirt, laying open fresh incisions like white lips, slicing deeper into muscle and bone.

See? Do I not bleed?

They won't listen.

I stagger from the embalming chamber, gouging my sides as I bump other caskets which topple, spilling their pale contents onto the mortuary floor.

My body is steaming as I stumble out into the cold, gray dawn.

Where can I go? What is left for me? There must be a place. There must be —

A bell chimes, and I awaken.

Frantically I locate the telephone.

A woman. Her voice is relieved but shaking as she calls my name.

"Thank God you're home," she says. "I know it's late. But I didn't know who else to call. I'm terribly sorry to bother you. Do you remember me?"

No luck this time. When? I wonder. How much longer?

"You can hear me," I say to her.

"What?" She makes an effort to mask her hysteria, but

I hear her cover the mouthpiece and sob. "We must have a bad connection. I'll hang up."

"No. Please." I sit forward, rubbing invisible cobwebs from my face. "Of course I remember you. Hello, Mrs. Richterhausen." What time is it? I wonder. "I'm glad you called. How did you know the number?"

"I asked Directory Information. I couldn't forget your name. You were so kind. I have to talk to someone first, before I go back to the hospital."

It's time for her, then. She must face it now; it cannot be put off, not anymore.

"How is your husband?"

"It's my husband," she says, not listening. Her voice breaks up momentarily under electrical interference. The signal re-forms, but we are still separated by a grid, as if in an electronic confessional. "At twelve-thirty tonight his, what is it, now?" She bites her lips but cannot control her voice. "His EEG. It ... stopped. That's what they say. A straight line. There's nothing there. They say it's nonreversible. How can that be?" she asks desperately.

I wait.

"They want you to sign, don't they, Emily?"

"Yes." Her voice is tortured as she says, "It's a good thing, isn't it? You said so yourself, this afternoon. You know about these things. Your wife ..."

"We're not talking about my wife now, are we?"

"But they say it's right. The doctor said that."

"What is, Emily?"

"The life-support," she says pathetically. "The Maintenance." She still does not know what she is saying. "My husband can be of great value to medical science. Not all the usable organs can be taken at once. They may not be matched up with recipients for some time. That's why the Maintenance is so important. It's safer, more efficient than storage. Isn't that so?"

"Don't think of it as 'life-support,' Emily. Don't fool yourself. There is no longer any life to be supported."

"But he's not dead!"

"No."

"Then his body must be kept alive ..."

"Not alive, either," I say. "Your husband is now — and will continue to be — neither alive nor dead. Do you understand that?"

It is too much. She breaks down. "H-how can I decide? I can't tell them to pull the plug. How could I do that to him?"

"Isn't there a decision involved in *not* pulling the plug?"

"But it's for the good of mankind, that's what they say. For people not yet born. Isn't that true? Help me," she says imploringly. "You're a good man. I need to be sure that he won't suffer. Do you think he would want it this way? It was what your wife wanted, wasn't it? At least this way you're able to visit, to go on seeing her. That's important to you, isn't it?"

"He won't feel a thing, if that's what you're asking. He doesn't now, and he never will. Not ever again."

"Then it's all right?"

I wait.

"She's at peace, isn't she, despite everything? It all seems so ghastly, somehow. I don't know what to do. Help me, please ..."

"Emily," I say with great difficulty. But it must be done. "Do you understand what will happen to your husband if you authorize the Maintenance?"

She does not answer.

"Only this. Listen: this is how it begins. First he will be connected to an IBM cell separator, to keep track of leucocytes, platelets, red cells, antigens that can't be stored. He will be used around the clock to manufacture an endless red tide for transfusions —"

"But transfusions save lives!"

"Not just transfusions, Emily. His veins will be a battleground for viruses, for pneumonia, hepatitis, leukemia, live cancers. And then his body will be drained off, like a stuck pig's, and a new supply of experimental toxins pumped in, so that he can go on producing antitoxins for them. Listen to me. He will begin to decay inside, Emily. He will be riddied with disease, tumors, parasites. He will stink with

fever. His heart will deform, his brain fester with tuber-
cules, his body cavities run with infection. His hair will fall,
his skin yellow, his teeth splinter and rot. In the name of
science, Emily, in the name of their beloved research."

I pause.

"That is, if he's one of the lucky ones."

"But the transplants..."

"Yes, that's right! You are so right, Emily. If not the
blood, then the transplants. They will take him organ by
organ, cell by cell. And it will take years. As long as the
machines can keep the lungs and heart moving. And
finally, after they've taken his eyes, his kidneys and the
rest, it will be time for his nerve tissue, his lymph nodes,
his testes. They will drill out his bone marrow, and when
there is no more of that left it will be time to remove his
stomach and intestines, as soon as they learn how to transplant those parts, too. And they will. Believe me, they will."

"No, please ..."

"And when he's been thoroughly, efficiently gutted —
or when his body has eaten itself from the inside out —
when there is nothing left but a respirated sac bathed from
within by its own excrement, do you know what they will
do then? *Do you?* Then they will begin to strip the skin from
his limbs, from his skull, a few millimeters at a time, for
grafting and re-grafting, until —"

"Stop!"

"Take him, Emily! Take your William out of there now,
tonight, before the technicians can get their bloody hands
on him! Sign nothing! Take him home. Take him away and
bury him forever. Do that much for him. And for yourself.
Let him rest. Give him that one last, most precious gift.
Grant him his final peace. You can do that much, can't you?
Can't you?"

From far away, across miles of the city, I hear the
phone drop and then clack dully into place. But only after I
have heard another sound, one that I pray I will never hear
again.

Goodspeed, Emily, I think, weeping. *Godspeed.*

I resume my vigil.

I try to awaken, and cannot.

3.

There is a machine outside my door. It eats people, chews them up and spits out only what it can't use. It wants to get me, I know it does, but I'm not going to let it.

The call I have been waiting for will never come.

I'm sure of it now. The doctor, or his nurse or secretary or dialing machine, will never announce that they are done at last, that the procedure is no longer cost-effective, that her remains will be released for burial or cremation. Not yesterday, not today, not ever.

I have cut her arteries with stolen scalpels. I have dug with an ice pick deep into her brain, hoping to sever her motor centers. I have probed for her ganglia and nerve cords. I have pierced her eardrums. I have inserted needles, trying to puncture her heart and lungs. I have hidden caustics in the folds of her throat. I have ruined her eyes. But it's no use. It will never be enough.

They will never be done with her.

When I go to the hospital today she will not be there. She will already have been given to the interns for their spinal taps and arteriograms, for surgical practice on a cadaver that is neither alive nor dead. She will belong to the meat cutters, to the first-year med students with their dull knives and stained cross sections ...

But I know what I will do.

I will search the floors and labs and secret doors of the wing, and when I find her I will steal her silently away; I will give her safe passage. I can do that much, can't I? I will take her to a place where even they can't reach, beyond the boundaries that separate the living from the dead. I will carry her over the threshold and into that realm, wherever it may be.

And there I will stay with her, to be there with her, to take refuge with her among the dead. I will tear at my body and my corruption until we are one in soft asylum. And there I will remain, living with death for whatever may be

left of eternity.
  Wish me Godspeed.

Dennis Etchison

THE LATE SHIFT

They were driving back from a midnight screening of *The Texas Chainsaw Massacre* ("Who will survive and what will be left of them?") when one of them decided they should make the Stop 'N Start Market on the way home. Macklin couldn't be sure later who said it first, and it didn't really matter, for there was the all-night logo, its bright colors cutting through the fog before they had reached 26th Street, and as soon as he saw it Macklin moved over close to the curb and began coasting toward the only sign of life anywhere in town at a quarter to two in the morning.

They passed through the electric eye at the door, rubbing their faces in the sudden cold light. Macklin peeled off toward the news rack, feeling like a newborn before the LeBoyer Method. He reached into a row of well-thumbed magazines, but they were all chopper, custom car, detective and stroke books, as far as he could see.

"Please, please, sorry, thank you," the night clerk was saying.

"No, no," said a woman's voice, "can't you hear? I want that box, *that* one."

"Please, please," said the night man again.

Macklin glanced up.

A couple of guys were waiting in line behind her, next

to the styrofoam ice chests. One of them cleared his throat and moved his feet.

The woman was trying to give back a small, oblong carton, but the clerk didn't seem to understand. He picked up the box, turned to the shelf, back to her again.

Then Macklin saw what it was: a package of one dozen prophylactics from behind the counter, back where they kept the cough syrup and airplane glue and film. That was all she wanted — a pack of Polaroid SX-70 Land Film.

Macklin wandered to the back of the store.

"How's it coming, Whitey?"

"I got the Beer Nuts," said Whitey, "and the Jiffy Pop, but I can't find any Olde English 800." He rummaged through the refrigerated case.

"Then get Schlitz Malt Liquor," said Macklin. "That ought to do the job." He jerked his head at the counter. "Hey, did you catch that action up there?"

"What's that?"

Two more guys hurried in, heading for the wine display. "Never mind. Look, why don't you just take this stuff up there and get a place in line? I'll find us some Schlitz or something. Go on, they won't sell it to us after two o'clock."

He finally found a six-pack hidden behind some bottles, then picked up a quart of milk and a half-dozen eggs. When he got to the counter, the woman had already given up and gone home. The next man in line asked for cigarettes and beef jerky. Somehow the clerk managed to ring it up; the electronic register and UPC Code lines helped him a lot.

"Did you get a load of that one?" said Whitey. "Well, I'll be gonged. Old Juano's sure hit the skids, huh? The pits. They should have stood him in an aquarium."

"Who?"

"Juano. It *is* him, right? Take another look." Whitey pretended to study the ceiling.

Macklin stared at the clerk. Slicked-back hair, dyed and greasy and parted in the middle, a phony Hitler moustache, thrift shop clothes that didn't fit. And his skin didn't look right somehow, like he was wearing makeup over a face that hadn't seen the light of day in ages. But Whitey was right. It was Juano. He had waited on Macklin too many times at that little Mexican restaurant over in East L.A., Mama Something's. Yes, that was it, Mama Carnita's on Whittier Boulevard. Macklin and his friends, including Whitey, had eaten there maybe fifty or a hundred times, back when they were taking classes at Cal State. It was Juano for sure.

Whitey set his things on the counter. "How's it going, man?" he said.

"Thank you," said Juano.

Macklin laid out the rest and reached for his money. The milk made a lumpy sound when he let go of it. He gave the carton a shake. "Forget this," he said. "It's gone sour." Then, "Haven't seen you around, old buddy. Juano, wasn't it?"

"Sorry. Sorry," said Juano. He sounded dazed, like a sleepwalker.

Whitey wouldn't give up. "Hey, they still make that good *menudo* over there?" He dug in his jeans for change. "God, I could eat about a gallon of it right now, I bet."

They were both waiting. The seconds ticked by. A radio in the store was playing an old '60's song. *Light My Fire,* Macklin thought. The Doors. "You remember me, don't you? Jim Macklin." He held out his hand. "And my trusted Indian companion, Whitey? He used to come in there with me on Tuesdays and Thursdays."

The clerk dragged his feet to the register, then turned back, turned again. His eyes were half-closed. "Sorry," he said. "Sorry. Please."

Macklin tossed down the bills, and Whitey counted his coins and slapped them onto the counter top. "Thanks," said Whitey, his upper lip curling back. He hooked a thumb in the direction of the door. "Come on. This place gives me the creeps."

As he left, Macklin caught a whiff of Juano or whoever he was. The scent was sickeningly sweet, like a gilded lily. His hair? Macklin felt a cold draft blow through his chest,

The Dark Country   **139**

and shuddered; the air conditioning, he thought.

At the door, Whitey spun around and glared.

"So what," said Macklin. "Let's go."

"What time does Tube City here close?"

"Never. Forget it." He touched his friend's arm.

"The hell I will," said Whitey. "I'm coming back when they change fucking shifts. About six o'clock, right? I'm going to be standing right there in the parking lot when he walks out. That son of a bitch still owes me twenty bucks."

"Please," muttered the man behind the counter, his eyes fixed on nothing. "Please. Sorry. Thank you."

The call came around ten. At first he thought it was a gag; he propped his eyelids up and peeked around the apartment, half-expecting to find Whitey still there, curled up asleep among the loaded ashtrays and pinched beer cans. But it was no joke.

"Okay, okay, I'll be right there," he grumbled, not yet comprehending, and hung up the phone.

St. John's Hospital on 14th. In the lobby, families milled about, dressed as if on their way to church, watching the elevators and waiting obediently for the clock to signal the start of visiting hours. Business hours, thought Macklin. He got the room number from the desk and went on up.

A police officer stood stiffly in the hall, taking notes on an accident report form. Macklin got the story from him and from an irritatingly healthy-looking doctor — the official story — and found himself, against his will, believing in it. In some of it.

His friend had been in an accident, sometime after dawn. His friend's car, the old VW, had gone over an embankment, not far from the Arroyo Seco. His friend had been found near the wreckage, covered with blood and reeking of alcohol. His friend had been drunk.

"Let's see here now. Any living relatives?" asked the officer. "All we could get out of him was your name. He was in a pretty bad state of shock, they tell me."

"No relatives," said Macklin. "Maybe back on the

reservation. I don't know. I'm not even sure where the —"

A long, angry rumble of thunder sounded outside the windows. A steely light reflected off the clouds and filtered into the corridor. It mixed with the fluorescents in the ceiling, rendering the hospital interior a hard-edged, silvery gray. The faces of the policeman and the passing nurses took on a shaded, unnatural cast.

It made no sense. Whitey couldn't have been that drunk when he left Macklin's apartment. Of course he did not actually remember his friend leaving. But Whitey was going to the Stop 'N Start if he was going anywhere, not halfway across the county to — where? Arroyo Seco? It was crazy.

"Did you say there was liquor in the car?"

"Afraid so. We found an empty fifth of Jack Daniel's wedged between the seats."

But Macklin knew he didn't keep anything hard at his place, and neither did Whitey, he was sure. Where was he supposed to have gotten it, with every liquor counter in the state shut down for the night?

And then it hit him. Whitey never, but never drank sour mash whiskey. In fact, Whitey never drank anything stronger than beer, anytime, anyplace. Because he couldn't. It was supposed to have something to do with his liver, as it did with other Amerinds. He just didn't have the right enzymes.

Macklin waited for the uniforms and coats to move away, then ducked inside.

"Whitey," he said slowly.

For there he was, set up against firm pillows, the upper torso and most of the hand bandaged. The arms were bare, except for an ID bracelet and an odd pattern of zigzag lines from wrist to shoulder. The lines seemed to have been painted by an unsteady hand, using a pale gray dye of some kind.

"Call me by my name," said Whitey groggily. "It's White Feather."

He was probably shot full of painkillers. But at least he was okay. Wasn't he? "So what's with the war paint, old buddy?"

"I saw the Death Angel last night."

Macklin faltered. "I — I hear you're getting out of here real soon," he tried. "You know, you almost had me worried there. But I reckon you're just not ready for the bone orchard yet."

"Did you hear what I said?"

"What? Uh, yeah. Yes." What had they shot him up with? Macklin cleared his throat and met his friend's eyes, which were focused beyond him. "What was it, a dream?"

"A dream," said Whitey. The eyes were glazed, burned out.

What happened? Whitey, he thought. Whitey. "You put that war paint on yourself?" he said gently.

"It's pHisoHex," said Whitey, "mixed with lead pencil. I put it on, the nurse washes it off, I put it on again."

"I see." He didn't, but went on. "So tell me what happened, partner. I couldn't get much out of the doctor."

The mouth smiled humorlessly, the lips cracking back from the teeth. "It was Juano," said Whitey. He started to laugh bitterly. He touched his ribs and stopped himself.

Macklin nodded, trying to get the drift. "Did you tell that to the cop out there?"

"Sure. Cops always believe a drunken Indian. Didn't you know that?"

"Look. I'll take care of Juano. Don't worry."

Whitey laughed suddenly in a high voice that Macklin had never heard before. *"He-he-he!* What are you going to do, kill him?"

"I don't know," he said, trying to think in spite of the clattering in the hall.

"They make a living from death, you know," said Whitey.

Just then a nurse swept into the room, pulling a cart behind her.

"How did you get in here?" she demanded.

"I'm just having a conversation with my friend here."

"Well, you'll have to leave. He's scheduled for surgery this afternoon."

"Do you know about the Trial of the Dead?" asked Whitey.

"Shh, now," said the nurse. "You can talk to your friend as long as you want to, later."

"I want to know," said Whitey, as she prepared a syringe.

"What is it we want to know, now?" she said, preoccupied. "What dead? Where?"

"Where?" repeated Whitey. "Why, here, of course. The dead are here. Aren't they." It was a statement. "Tell me something. What do you do with them?"

"Now what nonsense ...?" The nurse swabbed his arm, clucking at the ritual lines on the skin.

"I'm asking you a question," said Whitey.

"Look, I'll be outside," said Macklin, "okay?"

"This is for you, too," said Whitey. "I want you to hear. Now if you'll just tell us, Miss Nurse. What do you do with the people who die in here?"

"Would you please —"

"I can't hear you." Whitey drew his arm away from her.

She sighed. "We take them downstairs. Really, this is most ..."

But Whitey kept looking at her, nailing her with those expressionless eyes.

"Oh, the remains are tagged and kept in cold storage," she said, humoring him. "Until arrangements can be made with the family for services. There now, can we —?"

"But what happens? Between the time they become 'remains' and the services? How long is that? A couple of days? Three?"

She lost patience and plunged the needle into the arm.

"Listen," said Macklin, "I'll be around if you need me. And hey, buddy," he added, "we're going to have everything all set up for you when this is over. You'll see. A party, I swear. I can go and get them to send up a TV right now, at least."

"Like a bicycle for a fish," said Whitey. Macklin attempted a laugh. "You take it easy, now." And then he

The Dark Country   **143**

heard it again, that high, strange voice. *"He-he-he! tamunka sni kun."*

Macklin needed suddenly to be out of there.

"Jim?"

"What?"

"I was wrong about something last night."

"Yeah?"

"Sure was. That place wasn't Tube City. This is. *He-he-he!"*

That's funny, thought Macklin, like an open grave. He walked out. The last thing he saw was the nurse bending over Whitey, drawing her syringe of blood like an old-fashioned phlebotomist.

All he could find out that afternoon was that the operation wasn't critical, and that there would be additional X-rays, tests and a period of "observation," though when pressed for details the hospital remained predictably vague no matter how he put the questions.

Instead of killing time, he made for the Stop 'N Start.

He stood around until the store was more or less empty, then approached the counter. The manager, whom Macklin knew slightly, was working the register himself.

Raphael stonewalled Macklin at the first mention of Juano; his beady eyes receded into glacial ignorance. No, the night man was named Dom or Don; he mumbled so that Mackin couldn't be sure. No, Don (or Dom) had been working here for six, seven months; no, no, no.

Until Macklin came up with the magic word: police.

After a few minutes of bobbing and weaving, it started to come out. Raphe sounded almost scared, yet relieved to be able to talk about it to someone, even to Macklin.

"They bring me these guys, my friend," whispered Raphe. "I don't got nothing to do with it, believe me.

"The way it seems to me, it's company policy for all the stores, not just me. Sometimes they call and say to lay off my regular boy, you know, on the graveyard shift. 'Specially when there's been a lot of holdups. Hell, that's right

144

by me. I don't want Dom shot up. He's my best man!

"See, I put the hours down on Dom's pay so it comes out right with the taxes, but he has to kick it back. It don't even go on his check. Then the district office, they got to pay the outfit that supplies these guys, only they don't give 'em the regular wage. I don't know if they're wetbacks or what. I hear they only get maybe $1.25 an hour, or at least the outfit that brings 'em in does, so the office is making money. You know how many stores, how many shifts that adds up to?

"Myself, I'm damn glad they only use 'em after dark, late, when things can get hairy for an all-night man. It's the way they look. But you already seen one, this Juano-What-ever. So you know. Right? You know something else, my friend? They *all* look messed up."

Macklin noticed goose bumps forming on Raphe's arms.

"But I don't personally know nothing about it."

They, thought Macklin, poised outside the Stop 'N Start. Sure enough, like clockwork They had brought Juano to work at midnight. Right on schedule. With raw, burning eyes he had watched Them do something to Juano's shirt front and then point him at the door and let go. What did They do, wind him up? But They would be back. Macklin was sure of that. They, whoever They were. The Paranoid They.

Well, he was sure as hell going to find out who They were now.

He popped another Dexamyl and swallowed dry until it stayed down.

Threats didn't work any better than questions with Juano himself. Macklin had had to learn that the hard way. The guy was so sublimely creepy it was all he could do to swivel back and forth between register and counter, slithering a hyaline hand over the change machine in the face of the most outraged customers, like Macklin, giving out with only the same pathetic, wheezing *please, please, sorry, thank you,* like a stretched cassette tape on its last loop.

Which had sent Macklin back to the car with exactly no options, nothing to do that might jar the nightmare loose except to pound the steering wheel and curse and dream redder and redder dreams of revenge. He had burned rubber between the parking lot and Sweeney Todd's Pub, turning over two pints of John Courage and a shot of Irish whiskey before he could think clearly enough to waste another dime calling the hospital, or even to look at his watch.

At six o'clock They would be back for Juano. And then. He would. Find out.

Two or three hours in the all-night movie theatre downtown, merging with the shadows on the tattered screen. The popcorn girl wiping stains off her uniform. The ticket girl staring through him, and again when he left. Something about her. He tried to think. Something about the people who work night owl shifts anywhere. He remembered faces down the years. It didn't matter what they looked like. The nightwalkers, insomniacs, addicts, those without money for a cheap hotel, they would always come back to the only game in town. They had no choice. It didn't matter that the ticket girl was messed up. It didn't matter that Juano was messed up. Why should it?

A blue van glided into the lot.

The Stop 'N Start sign dimmed, paling against the coming morning. The van braked. A man in rumpled clothes climbed out. There was a second figure in the front seat. The driver unlocked the back doors, silencing the birds that were gathering in the trees. Then he entered the store.

Macklin watched. Juano was led out. The a.m. relief man stood by, shaking his head.

Macklin hesitated. He wanted Juano, but what could he do now? What the hell had he been waiting for, exactly? There was still something else, something else ... It was like the glimpse of a shape under a sheet in a busy corridor. You didn't know what it was at first, but it was there; you knew what it might be, but you couldn't be sure, not until you got close and stayed next to it long enough to be able to read its true form.

The driver helped Juano into the van. He locked the doors, started the engine and drove away.

Macklin, his lights out, followed.

He stayed with the van as it snaked a path across the city, nearer and nearer the foothills. The sides were unmarked, but he figured it must operate like one of those minibus porta-maid services he had seen leaving Malibu and Bel-Air late in the afternoon, or like the loads of kids trucked in to push magazine subscriptions and phony charities in the neighborhoods near where he lived.

The sky was still black, beginning to turn to slate close to the horizon. Once they passed a garbage collector already on his rounds. Macklin kept his distance.

They led him finally to a street that dead-ended at a construction site. Macklin idled by the corner, then saw the van turn back.

He let them pass, cruised to the end and made a slow turn.

Then he saw the van returning.

He pretended to park. He looked up.

They had stopped the van crosswise in front of him, blocking his passage.

The man in rumpled clothes jumped out and opened Macklin's door.

Macklin started to get out but was pushed back.

"You think you're a big enough man to be trailing people around?"

Macklin tried to penetrate the beam of the flashlight. "I saw my old friend Juano get into your truck," he began. "Didn't get a chance to talk to him. Thought I might as well follow him home and see what he's been up to."

The other man got out of the front seat of the van. He was younger, delicate-boned. He stood on one side, listening.

"I saw him get in," said Macklin, "back at the Stop 'N Start on Pico?" He groped under the seat for the tire iron. "I was driving by and —"

"Get out."

"What?"

"We saw you. Out of the car."

He shrugged and swung his legs around, lifting the iron behind him as he stood.

The younger man motioned with his head and the driver yanked Macklin forward by the shirt, kicking the door closed on Macklin's arm at the same time. He let out a yell as the tire iron clanged to the pavement.

"Another accident?" suggested the younger man.

"Too messy, after the one yesterday. Come on, pal, you're going to get to see your friend."

Macklin hunched over in pain. One of them jerked his bad arm up and he screamed. Over it all he felt a needle jab him high, in the armpit, and then he was falling.

The van was bumping along on the freeway when he came out of it. With his good hand he pawed his face, trying to clear his vision. His other arm didn't hurt, but it wouldn't move when he wanted it to.

He was sprawled on his back. He felt a wheel humming under him, below the tirewell. And there were the others. They were sitting up. One was Juano.

He was aware of a stink, sickeningly sweet, but with an overlay he remembered from his high school lab days but couldn't quite place. It sliced into his nostrils.

He didn't recognize the others. Pasty faces. Heads thrown forward, arms distended strangely with the wrists jutting out from the coat sleeves.

"Give me a hand," he said, not really expecting it.

He strained to sit up. He could make out the backs of two heads in the cab, on the other side of the grid.

He dropped his voice to a whisper. "Hey. Can you guys understand me?"

"Let us rest," someone said weakly.

He rose too quickly and his equilibrium failed. He had been shot up with something strong enough to knock him out, but it was probably the Dexamyl that had kept his mind from leaving his body completely. The van yawed, descending an off ramp, and he began to drift. He heard voices. They slipped in and out of his consciousness ilke fish in darkness, moving between his ears in blurred levels he could not always identify.

"There's still room at the cross." That was the younger, small boned man, he was almost sure.

"Oh, I've been interested in Jesus for a long time, but I never could get a handle on him ..."

"Well, beware the wrath to come. You really should, you know."

He put his head back and became one with a dark dream. There was something he wanted to remember. He did not want to remember it. He turned his mind to doggerel, to the old song. *The time to hesitate is through,* he thought. *No time to wallow in the mire. Try now we can only lose / And our love become a funeral pyre.* The van bumped to a halt. His head bounced off steel.

The door opened. He watched it. It seemed to take forever.

Through slitted eyes: a man in a uniform that barely fit, hobbling his way to the back of the van, supported by the two of them. A line of gasoline pumps and a sign that read WE NEVER CLOSE — NEVER UNDERSOLD. The letters breathed. Before they let go of him, the one with rumpled clothes unbuttoned the attendant's shirt and stabbed a hypodermic into the chest, close to the heart and next to a strap that ran under the arms. The needle darted and flashed dully in the wan morning light.

"This one needs a booster," said the driver, or maybe it was the other one. Their voices ran together. "Just make sure you don't give him the same stuff you gave old Juano's sweetheart there. I want them to walk in on their own hind legs." "You think I want to carry 'em?" "We've done it before, brother. Yesterday, for instance." At that Macklin let his eyelids down the rest of the way, and then he was drifting again.

The wheels drummed under him.

"How much longer?" "Soon now. Soon."

These voices weak, like a folding and unfolding of paper.

Brakes grabbed. The doors opened again. A thin light

The Dark Country   **149**

played over Macklin's lids, forcing them up.

He had another moment of clarity; they were becoming more frequent now. He blinked and felt pain. This time the van was parked between low hills. Two men in Western costumes passed by, one of them leading a horse. The driver stopped a group of figures in togas. He seemed to be asking for directions.

Behind them, a castle lay in ruins. Part of a castle. And over to the side Macklin identified a church steeple, the corner of a turn-of-the-century street, a mock-up of a rocket launching pad and an old brick schoolhouse. Under the flat sky they receded into intersections of angles and vistas which teetered almost imperceptibly, ready to topple.

The driver and the other one set a stretcher on the tailgate. On the litter was a long, crumpled shape, sheeted and encased in a plastic bag. They sloughed it inside and started to secure the doors.

"You got the pacemaker back, I hope." "Stunt director said it's in the body bag." "It better be. Or it's our ass in a sling. *Your* ass. How'd he get so racked up, anyway?" "Ran him over a cliff in a sports car. Or no, maybe this one was the head-on they staged for, you know, that new cop series. That's what they want now, realism. Good thing he's a cremation—ain't no way Kelly or Dee's gonna get this one pretty again by tomorrow." "That's why, man. That's why they picked him. Ashes don't need makeup."

The van started up.

"Going home," someone said weakly.

"Yes ... "

Macklin was awake now. Crouching by the bag, he scanned the faces, Juano's and the others'. The eyes were staring, fixed on a point as untouchable as the thinnest of plasma membranes, and quite unreadable.

He crawled over next to the one from the self-service gas stadon. The shirt hung open like folds of skin. He saw the silver box strapped to the flabby chest, directly over the heart. Pacemaker? he thought wildiy.

He knelt and put his ear to the box.

He heard a humming, like an electric wristwatch.

What for? To keep the blood pumping just enough so the tissues don't rigor mortis and decay? For God's sake, for how much longer?

He remembered Whitey and the nurse. *"What happens? Between the time they become 'remains' and the services? How long is that? A couple of days? Three?"*

A wave of nausea broke inside him. When he gazed at them again the faces were wavering, because his eyes were filled with tears.

"Where are we?" he asked.

"I wish you could be here," said the gas station attendant.

"And where is that?"

"We have all been here before," said another voice.

"Going home," said another.

Yes, he thought, understanding. Soon you will have your rest; soon you will no longer be objects, commodities. You will be honored and grieved for and your personhood given back, and then you will at last rest in peace. It is not for nothing that you have labored so long and so patiently. You will see, all of you. Soon.

He wanted to tell them, but he couldn't. He hoped they already knew.

The van lurched and slowed. The hand brake ratcheted.

He lay down and closed his eyes.

He heard the door creak back.

"Let's go."

The driver began to herd the bodies out. There was the sound of heavy, dragging feet, and from outside the smell of fresh-cut grass and roses.

"What about this one?" said the driver, kicking Macklin's shoe.

"Oh, he'll do his 48-hours' service, don't worry. It's called utilizing your resources."

"Tell me about it. When do we get the Indian?"

"Soon as St. John's certificates him. He's overdue. The crash was sloppy."

"This one won't be. But first Dee'll want him to talk,

The Dark Country   **151**

what he knows and who he told. Two doggers in two days is too much. Then we'll probably run him back to his car and do it. And phone it in, so St. John's gets him. Even if it's DOA. Clean as hammered shit. Grab the other end."

He felt the body bag sliding against his leg. Grunting, they hauled it out and hefted it toward—where?

He opened his eyes. He hesitated only a second, to take a deep breath.

Then he was out of the van and running.

Gravel kicked up under his feet. He heard curses and metal slamming. He just kept his head down and his legs pumping. Once he twisted around and saw a man scurrying after him. The driver paused by the mortuary building and shouted. But Macklin kept moving.

He stayed on the path as long as he dared. It led him past mossy trees and bird-stained statues. Then he jumped and cut across a carpet of matted leaves and into a glade. He passed a gate that spelled DRY LAWN CEMETERY in old iron, kept running until he spotted a break in the fence where it sloped by the edge of the grounds. He tore through huge, dusty ivy and skidded down, down. And then he was on a sidewalk.

Cars revved at a wide intersection, impatient to get to work. He heard coughing and footsteps, but it was only a bus stop at the middle of the block. The air brakes of a commuter special hissed and squealed. A clutch of grim people rose from the bench and filed aboard like sleepwalkers.

He ran for it, but the doors flapped shut and the bus roared on.

More people at the corner, stepping blindly between each other. He hurried and merged with them.

Dry cleaners, laundromat, hamburger stand, parking lot, gas station, all closed. But there was a telephone at the gas station.

He ran against the light. He sealed the booth behind him and nearly collapsed against the glass.

He rattled money into the phone, dialed Operator and called for the police.

The air was close in the booth. He smelled hair tonic. Sweat swelled out of his pores and glazed his skin. Somewhere a radio was playing.

A sergeant punched onto the line. Macklin yelled for them to come and get him. Where was he? He looked around frantically, but there were no street signs. Only a newspaper rack chained to a post. NONE OF THE DEAD HAS BEEN IDENTIFIED, read the headline.

His throat tightened, his voice racing. "None of the dead has been identified," he said, practically babbling.

Silence.

So he went ahead, pouring it out about a van and a hospital and a man in rumpled clothes who shot guys up with some kind of super-adrenalin and electric pacemakers and nightclerks and crash tests. He struggled to get it all out before it was too late. A part of him heard what he was saying and wondered if he had lost his mind.

"Who will bury them?" he cried. "What kind of monsters —"

The line clicked off.

He hung onto the phone. His eyes were swimming with sweat. He was aware of his heart and counted the beats, while the moisture from his breath condensed on the glass.

He dropped another coin into the box.

"Good morning, St. John's, may I help you?"

He couldn't remember the room number. He described the man, the accident, the date. Sixth floor, yes, that was right. He kept talking until she got it.

There was a pause. Hold.

He waited.

"Sir?"

He didn't say anything. It was as if he had no words left.

"I'm terribly sorry ..."

He felt the blood drain from him. His fingers were cold and numb.

"... But I'm afraid the surgery wasn't successful. The party did not recover. If you wish I'll connect you with —"

The Dark Country   **153**

"The party's name was White Feather," he said mechanically. The receiver fell and dangled, swinging like the pendulum of a clock.

He braced his legs against the sides of the booth. After what seemed like a very long time he found himself reaching reflexly for his cigarettes. He took one from the crushed pack, straightened if and hung it on his lips.

On the other side of the frosted glass, featureless shapes lumbered by on the boulevard, He watched them for a while.

He picked up a book of matches from the floor, lit two together and held them close to the glass. The flame burned a clear spot through the moisture.

Try to set the night on fire, he thought stupidly, repeating the words until they and any others he could think of lost meaning.

The fire started to burn his fingers. He hardly felt it. He ignited the matchbook cover, too, turning it over and over. He wondered if there was anything else that would burn, anything and everything. He squeezed his eyelids together. When he opened them, he was looking down at his own clothing.

He peered Out through the clear spot in the glass.

Outside, the outline fuzzy and distorted but quite unmistakable, was a blue van. It was waiting at the curb.

THE NIGHTHAWK

The little girl stood gazing north, toward the rich houses and the pier restaurant that was still faintly outlined through the mist. The high windows captured the white light of the sky in small squares, like a row of mirrors for the gulls; the pilings and struts underneath could have been stiff black legs risen from the sea and frozen in the November wind, never to walk again.

Is Maria coming? she wondered.

She had hurried to the corral first thing, of course, but Pebbles was gone. Maria must have come home early and taken him out, down past the big rocks to the Sea Manor, maybe, or up under the pier to the tidepools by the point at the edge of the Colony. She did not know what time Maria's school let out, had never asked, but still had always managed to be the first one home; she would be laying out the bridles or patching a break in the fence with driftwood from under the burned-out house by the time Maria came running — always, it seemed. Yes, always. Every time.

She began to wander back along the wet sand, found a stick and paused to block out a word in the sand — C-O-P-P-E-R — turning round over each letter and humming to herself to keep the chill away. But the fog came settling in now, a thick, tule fog it looked like, and she saw her breath making more fog in front of her face and so hastened the rest of the way with her head down, hearing only the cold breaking of the waves out on the dark, musseled rocks.

She stayed with Copper for as long as she could, leaving extra feed for Pebbles, too, so that Maria would not have to bother when she brought him back. Copper seemed restless, bobbing and pawing the sand, eager to be taken out. She tried to explain that it was too late now for a real ride and instead walked her out and around the cliffside and back, over the leach line creek that trickled from the cottages to the ocean. The tiny rivulet with its sculptured and terraced bed — she and Maria, trotting the ponies carefully from one crumbling tier to the other, liked to imagine that it was the Grand Canyon. But the truth was that she had no heart for riding, not now. Not with the dark coming on so soon and the fog all around. Not alone.

She was cold and growing colder as she climbed the wooden stairway and let herself in through the side door, the one to the storage room, and then slipped into the house as quietly as she could. She started to close the door on the fog, but decided to leave it ajar for Grandfather, who would probably be coming in soon.

She heard the television voices from the living room, the same ones she always heard when she went into the house after school. They laughed a lot, though there was an edge to the voices whenever they were interrupted by the music or the buzzer, which was almost all the time, it seemed. They were probably pretty nervous, too, about being kept on the program for so long, day after day, week after week; sometimes, of course, one of the voices would say the right things and win enough money to buy its freedom, and then they would have to let it go home and the next afternoon there would be another voice, a new one, to take its place. They always sounded excited and happy when they said a right answer, and then the audience would not laugh and the buzzer would not buzz.

She padded over the jute-covered floor and slipped around the doorway into the kitchen. She stopped with her hand on the refrigerator door. She looked back at the rattan chair and couch, the sandbag ashtrays, the clock and the flying metal geese on the wall, the shiny black panther on the table, the lamp shaped like a Hawaiian dancer, the ivy planter, the kissing Dutch girl and boy, the picture of the crying clown and the ones of the father and mother in the stand-up frames. She turned away. She opened the refrigerator and poured a glass of Kool-Aid.

"Is that you, Darcy?"

"Ye-es," she called sweetly, *Grandma,* but would not say it.

"Have you seen Maria yet?" She heard the grandmother climbing out of her chair, not waiting for an answer. "I must talk with you, dear. This morning we received a most disturbing telephone call ..."

The grandmother was coming, even though the TV was still on. It must be something bad, she thought.

On the other side of the kitchen window the fog was descending heavily, almost like rain. In fact she heard a tapping begin on the low roof — but no, that would be Grandfather, hammering with his short strokes, scraping his slippers on the rough tar paper. *Just a minute, I have to talk to Grandfather.* Would that be good enough? She turned from the window to watch the doorway for the black walking shoes, the hem of the flowered dress. Another kind of movement caught her eye, down low by the floor, but she knew that would only be the fog.

There was the hammering on the roof, the plinking of the wind chimes by the geraniums out on the railing of the sun deck, the fog deepening until it, too, could almost be heard settling over the house. There was the slow, unsteady pursuit of the grandmother, nearly upon her now.

And something else, something else.

A dull, familiar thumping.

She looked quickly and saw, through the window, a moving shape approaching along the beach. She knew at once that it was Pebbles. The pony hesitated, breathing steam, and the vapor thinned around him momentarily so that his markings showed clear and unmistakable, like a cluster of moonstones through the white water of a pool at low tide, far out by the broken sea wall.

"Got to go," she yelled, *Grandma.* "Maria's got Copper. Ooh, that girl —!"

She darted out and, by the time the refrigerator door had swung shut and before the grandmother could object, had dropped from the deck and was sprinting toward Maria and the pony. It wasn't true, of course; of course not. Maria was riding Pebbles. But it had worked.

"Hey," she called. Then, again, when there was no answer, "He-ey!"

Maria, small and dark atop her pony, reined and turned Pebbles, his hooves slapping the slick, packed sand. She had kept near the water, had not even come close to Darcy's house; but she had had to pass by on the way back, and now she held her body tense and distant, almost as though afraid she might meet something there on the beach — herself, say — with which she knew she would not be able to cope. "Hey, yourself," she said, because she had to say something. But her face did not change.

"Did you stay home today?" tried Darcy. She waited and, trying to make it look like she was not, had not been waiting, leaned forward and watched her feet as they dug down into the sand. She stepped back, and the imprints of her toes began to fill up with water. "Well, were you sick or something?"

"I got to go now," answered Maria.

She was like that. Once, when they were playing and Darcy had said something wrong — it must have been something she had said because nothing had happened, they had only been sitting with their knees up, molding little houses in the sand with a paper cup — Maria had stopped and stared over the water with that smooth, flat face of hers, as if hearing what no one else on the beach or in the world could hear. And then she had said that, the same thing, *I got to go now,* and she had jumped up, brushed off her hands and started running — and not even toward her own house, so that Darcy knew Maria hadn't been called home, even if she couldn't hear it herself. Maria was like that.

The pony started walking.

"You better not ride him anymore today, Maria," yelled Darcy. "Ma-ri-a, he'll get all sweaty and sick for sure, you'll see!"

Maria kept riding.

"Well," said Darcy, staring after, "*I* waited."

At the corral Maria dismounted but did not raise her eyes when her friend finally caught up.

"What do you care about Pebbles," Maria said to her.

Only then did Darcy notice the scratches, fresh and deep, on Pebbles' right flank. Three parallel lines sliced into flesh that was still pink and glistening.

Darcy sucked in her breath. "Maria!" She forgot everything else. "Who did *that?*"

Maria walked away. She trailed her fingers over the makeshift fence, the tarp that covered the hay, and went to sit in the ruins, in the shadows, under the starfish that someone had nailed crucifixion-style to the supports of the big house years ago, before it burned; now the hard, pointille arms, singed black at the tips, still clutched tight to the flaking, splintery wood. She put her elbows on her knees and her face in her arms and started to cry.

Copper had sidled over to Pebbles, but the other pony shied away, protecting his flank. Copper snorted and tried to nuzzle. Darcy reached for a blanket to throw over Pebbles, but hesitated because of the wound.

She joined her friend under the house.

After a time Darcy said, "I'll tell Grandfather. He'll get the vet to come over. You'll see."

"No."

Maria was crying deep down inside herself, from a place so protected that there were no sounds and nothing to show, nothing but the tears.

"Well, I'll go get some Zephiran right now from my house. And we'll fix it ourselves. I will, if you want me to, Maria."

"No!"

"Maria," she said patiently, "what happened?"

Maria's narrow lips barely moved. "It came. In the night, just like you said."

"What did?"

"You know what. The — the —"

"Oh no." Darcy felt a sinking inside, like an elevator going down too fast; she hadn't felt it for a long, long time. The last had been when she was very small, about the time that the mother and father went away. She couldn't remember the feeling very clearly; in fact, she couldn't even be sure what it was about; surely, she knew, it was about something she did not and could not understand. "Don't you be silly. It wasn't really real." That was right. It wasn't, it wasn't. "Maria, that was only a story. Ma-ri-a."

"That was what my Daddy said," the dark girl went on. "But he said you were still evil to make me scared of it." She was beginning to rush the words, almost as though afraid she might hear something and have to go away before she could finish. "You were the one, the one who told me about him, about how lie comes at night and sees in your window and if you were bad, then — you know. You know what he does, the Nighthawk."

The Nighthawk. Of course she remembered the story. It had always been just that, a story to scare children into being good, the kind of story thought up by grandmothers to stop too much running in the house and laughing and playing games in bed. But it was also a story you never forgot, and eventually it became a special late kind of story for telling on the beach, huddled close to a campfire, under the stars, seeing who could scare the other the worse, all shivery in sleeping bags, hidden from the unknowable mysteries of a sudden falling star or the sound of wings brushing the dark edge of the moon.

She didn't know what to say.

The two of them sat that way for a while.

"Well, I'll help you take care of him," she offered at last. "You know that."

"It doesn't matter."

"He'll be good as new. You'll see."

"Maybe. But not because of you."

Darcy looked at her friend as though seeing her for the first time.

Maria let out a long sigh that sounded like all the breaths she had ever taken going out at once. "My Daddy's getting a better place. Up in the canyon, by the real stables. He said Pebbles can't stay here till we find out what hurt him. And he says I can't play with you anymore."

"Why?"

"Because."

"But *why?*"

"Because you're the one who scared me of those stories." Her brown eyes were unreadable. "You can't tell me about the Nighthawk, Darcy," she said. "Not anymore, not ever again."

Darcy was stunned. "But I didn't make it happen," she said, her own eyes beginning to sting. "I don't even know what happened to Pebbles. Maybe he — well —" But she was confused, unable to think. She remembered the story from the mouth moving above her in the darkness as she huddled close to her big brother, a long, long time ago, it must have been. "Th-there isn't any real Nighthawk, don't you get it? Come on, I thought you were big! You know it, don't you? Don't you?"

"Don't *you?*" said Maria mockingly. "I don't want to have those dreams, like last night. Darcy, I don't want to!"

Darcy's mouth was open and stayed open as she heard a new sound, and it was not the blood pulsing in her ears and it was not the waves smashing out by the sea wall and it was not her own heartbeat. She looked over and saw Maria hunch down quickly, struggle to cover her eyes, then jerk herself up — almost wildly, Darcy thought later — as the sound became loud, louder. Darcy moved her lips, trying to be heard, trying to say that it was only one of those big Army helicopters somewhere above the fog, cruising low over the coastline — they were so much louder than the Sheriffs 'copter, their huge blades beating the air like some kind of monster — but Maria was already running. Just like that. In a few seconds she had disappeared completely in the fog.

Grandfather was sorting his tools when Darcy came up. She moved slowly, as though underwater, absently poking at a pile of ten-penny nails, at the chisel, at the claw of the hammer. She had been trying to think of where to begin, but it was no use.

"Well, how goes it today, sweetheart?' he said, when she made no move to go inside.

She knew he would wait to hear her story for today, whatever it might be, before getting around to the next part: the something that might be wrapped clean and special in a handkerchief in his jacket or lying inside on the kitchen table or, if it were another article about horses he had clipped from a magazine, folded and waiting in his shirt pocket. Then and only then would he get on to the serious part. She looked up at him and knew that she loved him.

"Oh —" She wanted to tell. Maybe if she started with a teacher story or a recess story; but she couldn't feel it. "Oh, same old stuff, I guess," she said.

He glanced at her, pausing perhaps a beat too long, and said, "The pictures came, the ones we sent away for in the Sunday *Times*. Those prints of the white stallions." He fixed her with his good eye. "Remember?"

She felt a smile beginning in spite of herself. She reached over to help him.

"And I believe your grandmother would like a word with you, Darcy, before you go downstairs."

"I know," she said quickly.

He latched his toolbox, wiped his hands on a rag.

Reluctantly she started inside.

"See you at dinner," he said. "Afterwards, we can measure them for frames and figure where they should go. All right?"

She turned back.

"Grandpa?"

"Yes?" He waited.

"What — what does it mean when somebody says you're 'evil'?"

He laughed easily.

"Well, Darcy," he said, "I'd have to say it just means that somebody doesn't really know you."

She felt her way downstairs. *Now do as you're told.* She made sure to land each foot squarely in the middle of each step. *I'm sure her father knows what's best, leaving it open to the air like that.* That way no part of her would touch the edge. *Remember — but of course you couldn't —* She was aware of a pressure at her heels. *Now why would you ask a thing like that, child? Why can't you leave well enough —* She knew what she would see were she to look back. *You'd better watch yourself, young lady. You're not too old to forget the —* She would see — *I didn't mean anything.* I didn't mean anything! *Your Mama and Daddy, rest their souls —* She would see the fog. *Say it.* Curling close. *Say It.* About her ankles. *Say it.* Say it —

"Help me."

She started.

Joel stood there in the semidarkness, one hand extended. The other hand was on the knob to the door next to hers, the door to his room. When her eyes adjusted, she saw that he held something out to her in his stubby fingers.

Without thinking, she took it. A pair of ringed keys, new and shiny. She studied them uncertainly.

Joel picked at a splinter along the doorjamb. As she watched, Darcy made out the bright brass gleam of a new lock.

"It's a dead-bolt," he said, as if that would explain everything. "Can't be forced, not unless you break the frame. The hinges are on the right side, too."

"But —"

"I want you to keep the keys in a safe place. Really safe. Got it?" When she nodded, he added with deceptive casualness, "You want to come in? You hardly ever do anymore, you know."

He opened the door and led her inside, looking like someone who had something terribly valuable to give away but could hardly remember where he had hidden it.

She hadn't seen the inside of her brother's room in weeks, maybe months. Since before she had met Maria. Usually they talked (more correctly, she listened while he talked) in her room, anyway, though, or else she managed to avoid him altogether to lie on her bed, playing her records or writing in her diary or thinking about the horses, the ones in the movie Grandfather had taken her to see, the wild ones leaping through water and fire on a seashore somewhere. It was very much like a dream.

While her own room seemed to be in a perpetual state of redecoration, Joel's remained the same jail-like no-color; where she had posters and cutouts to cover her walls, Joel had science and evolution charts and black felt-tip drawings she couldn't understand, marked up and shaded so dark that she couldn't see how he was able to make any sense of them. Still, it all reminded her of something, as it always did: she found herself thinking again about a house with unlocked doors and huge, loving faces bobbing in and out of the darkness over her. And fire, and water, and something else, something else.

The main thing she noticed, of course, was the statue on the shelf over the headboard of Joel's unmade bed. And, as before, it fascinated and frightened her at the same time.

It was a glazed plaster sculpture a couple of feet high, the paint brushed on real fast and sloppy, probably so that it could be sold cheap in the kind of stores that have pillows and ashtrays with words and pictures of buildings printed on them. Some kind of snake, a cobra, she thought, and it was coiled around what was supposed to be a human skull. Maybe it had come out of the skull, out of one of the eyes; she wasn't sure. But crawling out of the other eye was an animal that looked like a mouse. It was about to attack the snake, to try to bite it on the neck, or maybe to charm it, to hold its attention so that it would do no harm; she didn't know which. The snake was poised, squinting down, his fangs dripping. There was no way of telling which one would win. She had seen another like it once, in the window of a shop in the Palisades where they sold old-looking books and those sticks like Fourth of July punks that smell sweet when you light them. She wondered where Joel had gotten it and why and how much it cost, had even asked him one time, but he had only looked at her funny and changed the subject.

She sat on the edge of the bed.

"Joel," she began, knowing he would jump in about his locks and keys, whatever they were for, if she did not. There were things on her mind now, questions that were as yet only half-formed but which needed answers before she would be able to listen and really hear him. "Joel," she said again, trying to find a way to ease into it. "Was — was our house always this way? I mean, the way it is now? Or did Grandpa build it over when we were little?"

She glanced around the room, pretending interest in the cluttered walls and cramped ceiling.

"'Course it was," he said, casually condescending. "You're thinking about the other place."

"What other place is that, Joel?"

"The first house, the one over by your corral. The place where we lived with Mother and —"

He stopped himself, shot one of his sudden, funny looks at her, as if she had caught him off-guard.

She had an odd feeling then, as if they had begun to talk about something they were not supposed to, and her not even knowing. The feeling attracted her and scared her at the same time.

"You don't go poking around in there, do you?" he asked in a controlled voice. "Not all the way in there, where the house used to be?"

"Anyone can go, Joel. It's right there on the beach. What's left of it."

"You've been in there, underneath there? You've been there before?"

"I've *always* been there before. So what?"

He straightened, his back to her. "You shouldn't, you know. It's not safe."

"What do you mean? Of course it's —"

"There was an explosion once, you know," he said, cutting her off with more information than he had planned to give. "The gas lines are probably still there. Anyway, I don't want you remembering a thing like that. And," he added, as if to cover up, "you ought to stay home more."

"Oh."

She felt a laugh coming on, one of those wild, high ones that she didn't want to stop. She threw herself backwards on the bed, her arms over her head. His bed was so bouncy, mounded with all the quilts the grandmother had made for him.

"Safe, not safe," she sang. "Oh Joel, you're just on another one of your *bummers*. I know why you have such bad dreams. You pile on so many blankets, your body heats up at night like a compost heap!"

"Don't you taunt me, Darcy. Don't, or I'll —"

There, she had caught him again. *Or you'll what? Send the Nighthawk?*

He turned and stared at her for too long a time, until she stopped laughing and they both grew uneasy. Then he began moving about the room, picking at things, his compass and protractor, the lens cover to his telescope, putting them down again, pacing. It was an unnatural pause; Joel never ran out of crazy things to talk to her about, which was why she always had to be the one to leave.

He faced her again.

"I hear Grandma's pretty mad at you, Darcy." This time he was doing the taunting. The tension was gone from his face now, hidden again just below the surface like one of those sharp, crusted rocks when the tide changes. "What's it about this time?"

"Oh, who knows?" It was almost true; the grandmother was pretty nearly always mad at her about something. "I don't know, why is a mouse when it screams? That probably makes about as much sense." Then, when he didn't laugh, "It was about the ponies, I guess."

"What about the ponies?"

"What do you care?"

"I had a dream about them," he said tightly.

Another one of his dreams. She sighed. She didn't want to hear about it so she went ahead and told about Pebbles. But not the part about Maria. She was not ready to talk about that part yet, least of all to him.

But then she stopped and said, "It was about the corral, your dream, wasn't it? That was where you went. In your dream. *Wasn't* it."

Sometimes, she did not know why, Joel tried to make himself look like a stone boy; this was one of those times.

"Darcy, I tried to warn you. All of you." And, surprisingly, tears of rage came to his eyes. "I told him, I told *her* to tell him, but she must've thought she could take care of —"

A new thought struck her, cold and fully shaped as a steel bit, and it stayed and would not let go. Perhaps it had been there all along and only now was she able to feel it fully, its chill, and begin to know what it was.

She said, "What was it that hurt Pebbles?"

There was a ringing silence.

"You know, don't you, Joel. I think you know."

She saw him start to shake. She went on, oddly detached, as if she were watching what was happening through the wrong end of his telescope.

"You know what else I think? I — I think that maybe Mama and Daddy got hurt the same way, a long time ago. I already know they didn't just 'go away,' like everybody says."

She waited.

He did not try to answer. He lost his balance and hunkered close to the floor, by the edge of the bed. His hands clawed into the quilt and pulled it down with him.

Now she did begin to feel afraid. She felt a nervous jolt enter her body, sort of like a charge of static electricity from the air, but she strained to keep breathing, to draw energy from the feeling and not be smothered by it. She had to know.

"Say something!" she said to him.

She saw his face press into the pillow, heard his shallow, rasping sobs. She felt a terrible closeness in her own chest as her breath caught and took hold again. She thought of touching him but could not. Because she never had. Not like that.

"What about —" she began, and this was the hardest part, but it had to be said, "— what about the fire? Tell me about the fire, Joel. Tell me about Mother and Father."

I'll help you, I will, she thought, *and never, ever ask again. If only you'll tell me.* And then an answer came, slowly at first and then like something icy melting far away and rushing down to meet the sea. And whether it was his voice or her own she did not know just then, but could only focus on the pictures that appeared in her mind. And the pictures showed the big old house bursting upward into the sky and the boards falling back down again into a new and meaningless configuration on the sand, and she thought of charred pick-up-sticks. And before that: within the house a woman, breathing on her knees by the range, the oven open, the burners flickering and the image rising in a watery, gaseous mirage, and she thought *Mama.* And before that: a man dying in a hospital bed, his body laced with fresh scars, pink and glistening, and Mama weeping into her closed fists, her hair tumbling forward like brackwater and a little girl watching, and she thought *Daddy.* And before that: Daddy's face outside the window the night he brought Copper for her, smiling secretly and then the smile fading, shocked, as something, *something* moved against him beyond the glass, and she turned, turned for her brother who was not there, and she thought *the Nighthawk.* And before that: another face, dream-spinning over them both in the dark when Mama and Daddy were not home, an old face that went on storytelling long after she had fallen asleep, a face she had not let into her room since she had been old enough to lock it out, and again she thought *the Nighthawk.*

She stayed her hand in the air, near his head. Her voice was almost kind; her touch would have been almost cruel.

Outside, the tide was shifting. A single wave, the first of many, rolled and boomed against the retaining wall beneath the house. The bed throbbed once under her, and a pane of dirty glass in the one tiny window shook and rattled.

His head jerked up.

"No!"

"Shh," she said, "she'll hear you."

But of course it didn't matter. The grandmother wouldn't mind. She didn't mind anything Joel did, but only coddled him more. She waited on him, even in the middle of the night sometimes, with soothing cups of soup and those gray-and-red pills that were supposed to be hidden in the back of the top shelf of the medicine cabinet. And if Grandfather heard or cared, he wouldn't do anything about it, either. He left the boy alone, no matter what, to dream his dreams and become what he would. Of course it was silly to think that Grandfather would be — what? afraid of him? Of course it was. He was only a boy. He was only her brother Joel.

She followed his gaze to the window. The water was rolling in long, slow curls, tipped at the ebb with a pearly-white phosphorescence. But Joel wasn't seeing that.

For the first time she noticed the window sill.

It was scored with dozens, hundreds of vertical cuts and scratches; the marks shifted and deepened as she watched, as Joel's shadow undulated over the scarred wood. Then she glanced back and saw the burning aureole of the high-intensity lamp behind him, across the room, the one the last tutor, who had stayed the longest, had left on his final visit.

Without warning, Joel lurched up. He stood a moment, turned around, around again, in the manner of an animal who has awakened to find himself trapped in a room with the door shut and the air being sucked from his lungs. Whatever he was looking for he did not see, or even, probably, know how to name it, because just then he did a strange thing, really: he shrank down until he was sitting on the floor, right where he had been standing, without

The Dark Country   **169**

having moved his feet at all. She had seen something like that only once before. It had been the day the grandmother came home from what Darcy knew had been the funeral for the father and mother; it was as if she now had permission to remember. The grandmother had come in cradling two armloads of groceries. She had stood in the middle of the kitchen, scanning the walls like that, not seeing any of it, least of all the little girl there in the doorway, because Darcy was not what she was looking for, any more than the walls or ceiling or the table and chairs. And she had moved from side to side, turning from the waist, and then the expression had come over her face and she had sunk down onto the linoleum, the bags split and the contents rolling, forgotten, a collapsed doll with its strings cut. She had probably not even known that Darcy was there.

"Use the key," he said to her, "now."

"Why?"

"Do it, Darcy."

She stepped around him carefully and backed to the door.

She saw the way the light played over the sculpture above the bed. The way its eyes shone, forever straining but unable to see the most important thing of all. The way the shadow had grown behind the hood, so that it had come to be larger, darker, more like the monster from a bedtime story than she had ever noticed. She found herself staring into the eyes until she seemed to recognize something; yes, she herself remembered the way it felt, the need to lash out and hurt. What would have happened to her those times if she had not had Grandfather there to help? And there was something else, too, about a snake she had seen in a book, one that had gotten so mad or afraid that it had actually tried to swallow its own tail ...

The eyes held her longer than she liked. The sharp eyes that missed nothing, not the other creatures that had come close enough to threaten, not the head that had nurtured it but which was now too old and empty to protect it, not anything but itself, what it had become, the very thing it feared most, the creature of its dreams, the most difficult thing of all to know when the dreams it is given are all nightmares.

She was standing between the door and the lamp. The shadow of Joel's head and body moved and distorted. She drew back involuntarily and, behind her back, her hand brushed the cold doorknob.

She shuddered.

She imagined the fog creeping down the steps from outside, hissing over the floor and pooling by the edges. She pushed the door shut and moved away.

As she moved, her own shadow merged with the other, rendering it somehow less frightening. But the eyes on the headboard shimmered and burned out of the blackness, and she wanted to say, *Does it see, Joel?*

He gestured at her imploringly.

She wished she could say *I got to go now,* the way Maria would have said it, and simply run away as fast as she could. But there was the dark outside, and the fog that followed her down the stairs, waiting to slither under doors and between cracks. There was the grandmother, she knew, waiting at the top of the stairs with her words, her stories that would not soothe but only bring more nightmares. She wondered whether the grandmother knew that; probably not, she realized, and that was the most frightening thought of all.

She went to him.

"What do you want me to do, Joel?"

Suddenly she felt her wrist taken in a death grip.

"No, Joel, not me!" she cried, wrenching free. She lunged for the door. "I'm doing it, see, I'm ..."

She reached up to lock the door, thinking, *Why did he give me both keys?* But it was a good idea to lock it now, yes, she would —

She stared at the door.

Where was the lock? The mechanism was on the outside, as were the hinges. So the keys could not be used to keep anything out.

They could only be used to lock something in.

Very slowly she came back to him, his unblinking eyes

following her.

"What do you see, Joel?" she said softly.

There was the room. The window. The luminous waves, aglow now with the pale, dancing green of St. Elmo's fire rippling below the surface. The sky ablaze with a diffused sheen of moonlight above the fog. The glass chill and brittle now, and if she placed her fingers on it they would leave behind five circles imprinted in mist, the record of a touch that would remain to return each time someone sat close and breathed at the night.

Then she was listening to the slapping of the surf, the trembling in the close room, the sound of a sob and the high, thin weeping of the wind, that might have been the keening of an animal left too long alone.

"Do you hear that, Joel? Is that Copper?"

And she saw the room and that it was only her brother's, and she heard the crying and knew that it came from her own lips, and she reached out her hand to him and felt his moist hair, the bristles at the back of the neck, the fuzz at his temple and the quivering in his cheek and the wetness running to and from his tender mouth and the shaking of his body.

Closing her eyes, she said, "How do you feel?"

He would have told her to go away, just to go away and lock the door and not open it until the morning. But she placed herself between him and the window and said:

"I'm going to stay, Joel. I want to. I'll watch and listen from here and if anyone — if Copper — needs me, I'll know it. Do you understand?"

"No," he said pitifully, after some time had passed.

She kept her eyes shut tight against the fog and the world as she said, "It's all right. I'm only waiting, Joel, for you to go to sleep."

Because, she thought, somebody has to.

And that was the way their first real night together began.

IT WILL BE HERE SOON

1/ Something Strange in Santa Mara

It was a time of leisure and deadly boredom, of investigation and inconclusion, of heat waves and chills under an effluvial sky; of cancer research and chemical juggernauts, of Tac Squads and the Basic Car Plan, of God freaks and camper cities; of no longer suppressed unrest. Assassination, mass murder, ascension to office; the bomb in the backyard and the cop in the woodpile.

Still, had Martin been able to love anyone, he would have loved his father.

"Santa Mara's not what it used to be," Martin's father was saying.

The older man rubbed his hands and glanced around the garage, almost as though expecting to see himself walk in at any moment. Boxes of many sizes were barricaded on the cement floor, some with their flaps tied upright with twine in the style of old-time grocery carry-outs. Poking out of the boxes was an uncatalogable array of picture tubes (dusty), plastic knobs, tuners, dials, tube testers, transformers, radios, cabinet legs, schematics, speaker cones (broken), screws, capacitors, battery chargers, resistors, screwdrivers, manuals, transistors, wire strippers, solder rolls (sagging), sockets, relays, short wave sets, circuit breakers, wrenches, epoxy, white box tape, panels, power cords (frayed), pliers, coils, flywheels, oscilloscopes, wire cutters, washers, templates, heat sinks, mica sheets (cracked), motors, switches, circuit boards, nuts, magnets, friction tape, fuses, vacuum tubes — a detritus of years accumulated privately, away from the light of day.

From the single screened window filtered a hissing sound, as the mother watered her rosebushes one last time.

"So," began Martin uneasily. "How's the new house coming?"

"Oh, your mother — Henny, I mean — was out there yesterday for the pouring of the concrete. You have to watch things with a mobile home. The dirt's got to be packed right. Otherwise the first rain'll sink it all in and burst the pipes. I should have gone out. But this damned numbness has been getting to me." He massaged his left arm absently. "See, you have to make sure she's leveled right from the start, before you let them put the skirting around. There are so many things. Let me tell you." He sighed. It sounded like all the breaths he had ever drawn going out at once.

Martin gave up trying to count the boxes. "What's going to happen to all this?"

"Oh, she's got it figured. The park association's promised us a tool shed on the back. I'll have to use that for my workshop, I guess. Meanwhile, there's the storage locker. I put a check in the mail today. Two months in advance."

Martin looked at his fingernails. Somewhere down the block, puppies were yelping.

"Hallendorfs," said his father. "They never let up, ever since."

He cleared his throat. "How is old Pete, anyway?"

His father glanced up with tired eyes.

"He never made it home, Jack. In there the same time I was, you know. Different floor."

"I didn't know, Dad. I'm sorry."

Martin felt his father's eyes on him.

"Jackie? *Do you know the way to Santa Mara?*"

He tried to read his father's meaning, studying his face like a problem book from which the answer page has been torn out. "I guess I do, Dad," he said finally. He tried to laugh. "I made it here, didn't I?"

His father was smiling strangely. "Good." He leaned forward conspiratorially. "That was why they didn't let him out, you know." He nodded once, as if he had made a point.

"Is that right?"

"I'll tell you, though. There's something that *I* know."

Martin waited.

"I know that Santa Mara's not what it used to be. It never was."

2/ Wiggle Alley

Going through Wiggle Alley opens gates
Hitting bumper when lit activates flipouts
Going into moving hole starts rollovers
Spelling out name of game closes flippers
EXTRA points on last shot scores SPECIAL

———

One, Two, or More Players
It's Fun to Compete!

Martin hated bowling alleys.

He left the pinball machine, turned over three (or was it four?) drinks in the lounge and then slipped out through the glass door, closing off the ringing of the machine and the cries of children, the clicking of disposable cocktail tumblers, the clapping of the Thursday Nite League down on the lanes and the clattering work of the automatic pin-spotters — a dull and numbing sound, something between the thud of vinyl and the knock of real wood.

He got into his car and drove back across town, passing the old Seventh Day Adventist campground on the way; he saw that sometime since his last visit to Santa Mara it had been cleared and a Zody's Discount Department Store put up in its place.

He passed the park, slowing by the picnic tables. Beyond the firepits the old natatorium still stood; he noticed that most of the high windows had been broken out by vandals, so that the building now appeared somehow foreboding, the jagged remnants of panes reflecting the night breeze's strafing of the cold waters inside.

He passed the war memorial cannon, and almost stopped there. Had he, as a child, ever carved his initials into the gray paint? He couldn't remember. As he drew alongside, he saw that it had been decorated with a dark, intricate pattern. Then he recognized the matrix as a web of spray-can gang writing. It covered everything. He could not make out any of the hieroglyphs.

He drove on.

He passed many vaguely familiar tree-shrouded streets, but did not turn into any of them.

He felt a wall of sound before he heard it, and knew that he was near the new freeway. He geared down through the underpass and, after a couple of instinctive turns, found himself coasting into the driveway. *Thump*. There, now he had done it. Done something. But it was only the mailbox — he had clipped it with his front fender. No damage. But he realized that he did feel something from the drinks, after all.

He cut the ignition. The engine ticked, cooling down, as he sat staring into the familiar shrubbery at the front of the house. Jasmine, he remembered. There had been night-blooming jasmine.

He got out of the car.

Down the block, the puppies were crying again. He headed for the back door, but before he got to it he heard something else: a switching, scissoring sound, as of blades.

He squinted into the darkness.

Near the end of the street, a dimly-outlined figure pushed what looked like a lawn mower to the sidewalk, turned and disappeared back into the shadows.

Hell of an hour, he thought. And shivered. It was turning late in the year, and the breeze he felt would soon be a wind. He fumbled for his old door key under the planter.

176

Leaves caught at his hands and face. He knew the scent. It wasn't jasmine. It was oleander.

He sat at the table in the empty kitchen, the light reflecting off the enameled walls and stripped floor.

He was trying to understand. Something was missing, all right. What exactly was it that he was supposed to feel?

There was a book on the table. He reached for it. It was mimeographed, stapled, with a hand-lettered cover. *Class of '61, Fifteen Year Reunion, Disneyland.* It must have come in the mail and been left out for him by the mother. She had probably thought he would toss it out unopened, if he saw it first. She was right.

Why *had* he gone to the bowling alley, anyway? Even as a teenager he had hated it — yet tonight he had gone there. And he had felt let down.

Why?

He slapped the table.

The machine. He remembered. Absurdly, there had been only four balls, instead of five, in the pinball machine.

He laughed bitterly. He leaned forward and squeezed his eyes shut; when he opened them again the lashes stuck together wetly. Crazy bastard, he thought, you poor, crazy bastard.

He knew why he had gone there.

He had wanted to make some kind of contact. One of the girls, perhaps, who had stayed on in Santa Mara. Who had been waiting all these years for someone to come back and — what? Take her away? Take her to a motel? He riffled the pages of the book. The telephone was there on the wall. The information operator would give him a number. If he could just remember a name. He opened the book, reached for the phone.

His father shuffled into the kitchen.

"Jack," he said, nodding formally. "Thought that might be you." He sighed and sank into a chair. "Couldn't sleep. Do you suppose," he said, "that you might be up to listening to your old man yap for a while?"

The Dark Country   **177**

3/ Talking Heads

"There's a lot of things I haven't told anyone, Jack," he said, leading the way into the unlighted living room. "Least of all her."

Martin waited by the couch. His father went ahead and sank into the overstuffed cushions. He heard a groan, but couldn't tell whether it was the couch or not. He sat on the arm. His father handed him the television remote control.

"You ever try any of those *psychedelics,* Jack?" It sounded as if he were saying the word for the first time; as he spoke, he motioned at the TV set.

Martin felt for the ON button. "You mean LSD, that sort of thing?"

A used-car salesman with freeze-dried hair flickered to life on the screen. Martin left the sound down.

"You don't have to answer, of course. The reason I bring it up —" He stopped. He glanced around, his eyes settling on the doorway that led to the dark hall and the bedrooms. Then he put a finger to his lips, cupped a hand behind his· ear and motioned at the set again.

Martin understood. He eased up the volume control until it was just loud enough to mask their voices.

His father chuckled sourly at the salesman. "Look at that son of a bitch, will you," he said. "Those teeth. Like he's ready to eat us right where we sit. Hand me the heating pad, will you, son? I think you're sitting on it."

Martin smiled and felt for the cord. *Son of a bitch.* He was mildly surprised; he could not remember hearing his father talk that way before today. Of course it didn't matter anymore. It must feel good for him, he thought.

His father muttered and pushed himself up, but instead of plugging in the heating pad he went to the corner, to some packing cartons, and rummaged about. The commercial ended, the program resumed: it was Chuck Ashman, the local columnist, in the midst of another of his late-night interviews. His father came back to the couch, arms full.

He handed Martin a pair of headphones. In the frosty television light, Martin recognized a tape deck and a stack of hand-labeled cassettes.

Everything's changing, slipping out from under him since the operation, the forced retirement, he thought. And now the move. So what if he's a little — what? Eccentric? Was that a word he could use about his father? Well, at least he isn't senile; whatever he is, he certainly has a right to it.

There was a new Dolbyized tape deck, an expensive one, microphones, patch cords and all the accessories. It was a better system than Martin had back at the apartment; in fact, he realized with a sinking feeling, he didn't even have his audio equipment anymore, not since Kathy had cleaned out the place. He hadn't even contested the settlement.

"Looks like a pretty sweet set-up, Dad."

"These," his father said with quiet intensity, "are the tools of my research. At least that's what I call them," he added self-deprecatingly. He leaned back, waiting.

Martin handled the tapes uncertainly. The labels were dated, going back about six months — about the time his father had come home from the hospital — and all were marked *Raudive-Sheargold meth., mic.,* followed by anywhere between one and a dozen check marks.

"You know anything about Voices, Jack?"

He looked up. His father indicated a collection of books, magazines, and newspaper clippings on the coffee table. One of the books was titled *Voices from the Tapes,* another *Unpopular Science.* He also recognized a copy of *FATE* and an old *National Enquirer.*

He suppressed a grin. So this was the sort of thing the old man was getting into now. He couldn't believe it. He vaguely recalled going into Los Angeles to hear Gabriel Greene lecture about his meetings with the "space people" many, many years ago, about the time he had been going through his science fiction paperback phase, but seemed also to remember that he had had almost literally to drag

his father along. In fact, the man had always been method-
ical, even hidebound in his thinking; the lifelong interest in
electronics, the sparetime correspondence courses — that
had been quite the right kind of hobby for such a careful,
logical mind. But now this.

"I'd like to hear about it, Dad."

The old man propped his hands behind his head and
began speaking, staring into the TV and past it. He warmed
to the subject slowly, point by point, but soon his voice was
coming fast and hoarse, his words clipped, his white hands
describing in the air. The gist of it went something like this:

In '64, a certain naturalist had been trying out a new
tape machine to record bird songs in the field; during playback, his Great Dane pricked up its ears at portions of the
tape where nothing was audible, at least to the human ear
(his master's voice?). A boost in amplification revealed a
faint, barely intelligible voice above the background noise,
one with a peculiar, rhythmic, otherworldly cant to it that
was soon to become familiar. There then followed other sci-
entists, laboratories, experiments, miles of magnetic tape,
and before long "Spirit Voice Phenomena" had been verified; a new movement was born. And so on. With a
straight face, Martin's father explained how he believed
"the Voices" to be evidence of intelligent beings beyond the
physical plane.

"... And there's Dr. Raudive in Germany, who has
recordings of 72,000 *different voices.*"

Martin's attention was wandering, but he tried at least
to follow the drift. A fleck of spittle flew from his father's
mouth; it reminded him of a moth. He didn't quite know
how to take all this, though he presumed he was supposed
to take it quite seriously.

"You record with the gain full up. That's Sheargold's
method. I can only do it when she's not around. You can
imagine what doors slamming, dishes sound like ..."

"So. Let me see if I follow. You rewind the tapes then,
and —"

"Right. I monitor each reel, at different levels, through
the Koss headset. And chromium dioxide tape, which is

what this machine is biased for. Condenser mikes, of course."

Of course. And does he actually hear things? wondered Martin. Well, maybe so. Maybe he does.

"What's turned up so far?"

His father plugged the phones into the machine, inserted a cassette from the top of the stack and started the PLAY button.

"You tell me," he said. "You might be able to help, Jack. If you're inclined to. I haven't gone over this one yet."

Martin shrugged and slipped the phones over his ears. It began with the sound of his father's voice: his name, the date — yesterday, "one forty-six p.m., Santa Mara, California" — and then a regular, unending hiss as the recorded volume went all the way up. Even in the Dolby playback mode, the surface noise was harshly audible. Like sticking your head in a giant conch shell, he thought.

He closed his eyes, straining to hear a pattern in the wash of white sound, but it only wound on, steady and unchanging, like a perpetual ebbing of water. He began to think of the microscopic particles of oxide passing under the sounding head of the deck as grains of sand on a wide, endless stretch of beach. No voices, horns, telephones, alarms; only peace. He felt the cushion beneath him rise and fall, like the earth itself and its tides rocking his weight through a merciful, dreamless sleep.

He thought he detected a low drone under the susurrus. Then a flash of light danced on his eyelids as the TV screen shifted images across the dark room. He opened his eyes.

He tried to focus. His father's lips were moving. In the half-light, the lips had a bluish, ghostly tinge. He uncupped the phones from his head; the ear cushions broke their seal with a pop.

"... Every night, about this time. Every night. As close to me as that door." The old man raised a pale finger and pointed toward the hall.

Martin couldn't know how much he had missed. He waited, but the old man did not go on.

He cleared his throat. "So," he tried, feeling disoriented. "What — how was it that you got started in all this?"

Eyes fixed ahead, his father said, "Kathy left some books for me at the hospital, that time she drove out from the city. One of the times you couldn't make it. Business meeting or something," he said distantly, without recrimination, as if talking about a different life. "Yes sir, I knew I had to try to make contact as soon as I got out. After what happened."

Martin's heart sank as, unexpectedly, he found himself overwheimed with guilt. *I never made it out to visit, not once while he was in there. But Kathy did. Of course. She would. That was like her. Buttering people up, maintaining every appearance ... and then, one day, poof. Gone. Just like that. That was her way. She wasn't really cold — merely cowardly.* She left some books. *Which ones?* Unpopular Science? *Had she meant it as a dig at the old man's love of real scientific research? No, she wasn't that subtle. In her way, maybe she had actually believed he would want to read about some of her off-the-wall fads. Shiatzu, lecithin, pyramid power, plants that talk. The irony was that this time the someone who had given her the benefit of the doubt was his own father. He wondered if she knew that. Was she gloating over it now in some ashram or teepee or wherever the hell she and her latest curly-headed guru were getting it on?*

"You don't suppose she wants them back, do you?"

What? The books? He did know that the two of them had shot their wad, didn't he? Is he that far out of it, then?

He was beginning to get a feeling he didn't know how to name. But he had to pursue it. "Dad, what was it you were getting at before, when you asked me about drugs? LSD, that sort of thing. Remember?"

"Mm. I sure thought I was high, let me tell you. The whole time I was in there. I thought I was on some kind of *trip.*"

"What kind of medication were you getting? You know, they must have kept you pumped full of something after the surgery."

"Oh, I asked the doctor. Painkillers, he said. That's all, just painkillers."

Martin considered. "I've heard experiences like that aren't all that rare. I mean, you were probably running a fever, hallucinating —"

"I might have thought the same as you at first. But then they started coming for me. Every night, right at midnight, whether I was asleep or not. Of course, after the first few times, I made a point of staying awake."

Again Martin seemed to have missed something. "Who?"

There was a pause. "I wish I knew the words to describe them."

"I wish you'd try."

"Mm. Let's just see here once. They were dressed in one-piece outfits, what do you call them? Tunics. They had faces that were smooth and just-not-human. They might have been, but they weren't."

"They — they came into your room?"

"From the walls. They came out of the wardrobe. They'd stand and watch. Waiting. I thought they wanted me to go with them."

Good lord, he thought.

"Couldn't hear. They'd laugh and point at my cast. Mocking, I guess, because I didn't get it. Finally I figured they had to be communicating on some other frequency. As soon as I find it ... Tomorrow maybe I'll rig an RF choke to a 100,000 ohm resistor, with a diode instead of a mike coupled direct into the recorder. Jack," he said, leaning forward, with a charged intensity that filled the room with an almost palpable presence. "Jack, they were trying to tell me something. Do you understand me? They managed to leave a part of it on my cast, don't ask me how. Did I tell you that? Look at that one, will you?"

On the screen, the interview was still in progress. Opposite Ashman sat one of the most bizarre-looking beings Martin had ever set eyes on. Out of a reflex curiosity he moved to turn up the volume, when an identifying caption appeared over the face:

MIKEL
Member of Rock Group
"Cycle Sluts"

They continued to watch the silently moving lips.

"He could be one," said the old man. He even chuckled. "As well as anyone, I suppose. Who knows?" Then he said, "Maybe I'm just getting old."

Martin turned his head, trying to see his father's eyes in the dim light.

"I must be. Trying to get through to them. But, you know, sometimes I think it's the only thing that keeps me going.

"She got it in her head to move. I can't fight. She says there'll be 'luxury' out there. Less upkeep. There'll be less to do, all right. I can tell you. I'll knock around inside that trailer like a loose lugnut. Don't even know if I'll be able to keep up with the research out there. Of course, after a while, who knows? Maybe I won't even want to."

His voice took on an incantatory rhythm.

"You know what it'll be like? I'll tell you. It'll be just the same as it was here on sick leave, before the operation. Get up. Can't sleep past dawn, anyway. Putter around. Watch TV. Take a walk. Take a nap. Sit around waiting for dinner. More TV, go to bed. Get up again, try to watch Tom Snyder. Go back to bed. Can't talk to her — never could. I don't know what she wants from me, I swear I don't.

"She sure as hell doesn't want me to move my old radios and the rest of it, I know that. Well, she got her way — but only for the time being. They're going into storage. I'm paying for that with my own money. Until we get the spare room.

"She had some of it packed away before I got home from the hospital. Did you know that?"

They sat side by side, not looking at each other. Crickets started up outside. It grew very late.

"To tell the truth, I haven't tinkered with my old sets

184

for a long time. Since way before the accident. God knows, maybe it'll get to be like that with the research. Maybe I never will hear them, after all. Maybe the ones who say they do are on some kind of trip. Or it's a function of the equipment. I guess I have to admit that. Don't I, Jack." It wasn't a question.

Martin felt words caught in his throat.

"You know why I stopped listening to my old sets?" his father said. "I'll tell you. Because they don't sound as good as they used to. They just don't sound the same at all."

The old man rose and moved slowly across the room, toward the television set and the door to the hall. When he spoke again, the voice sounded far away, getting farther, and very tired.

"I was thinking you could help me, son. The research. No, that's right, you have to go back to your work, your own life tomorrow. I understand. It was good of you to come out and help us pack. The movers are taking care of everything. We won't have to lift a finger. It was good of you, though."

He turned back.

"Why do you suppose that is? The old sets, I mean. Why don't they sound like they used to?"

I know why. It's the programs. They aren't the same as they used to be. They aren't the same programs, he thought, and they aren't as good. But he didn't say it. He didn't say anything. He couldn't.

4/ All Screaming, All Bleeding, All Dying

A recap of the news came on the all-night channel; at some point the newscast became something called "Creature Features," this week presenting a double bill of Italian or German horror movies of the sleaziest kind, their screaming and bleeding and dying badly dubbed into English and interrupted every seven minutes or so for repetitions of a commercial spot for a recreational vehicle dealership.

Unaccountably, he began to feel that he was being watched. He left the set on.

He passed into the dream as easily as a breath is taken and released. He was aware of the street lamp outside the window, the lights in the last houses along the block finally winking off, the passing and re-passing of cars on the empty street, the easy silence, and the night.

He found himseif stranded at the outskirts of an unknown city. He had forgotten what he was doing there, who had left him, when or if it would ever return. From time to time he froze in his tracks, aware of the long umbilical by which he was attached to an electrical outlet, he did not know where. He worked his way through rubble, picking over piles of rags and discard, even though he could no longer remember what it was he was looking for. The sky grew ripe. A panic began to swell in his chest. There was a loosening, a sag and then he felt it slip away and he could not move. Time passed. His kidneys ached with the dull throb of fear. Time was running out. With monumental effort, with the last of the residual energy in his synapses, he strained his fingers to his pockets. He handled crystals, connectors, the myriad spare parts he always carried with him, feeling for the right pieces with which to effect a repair. Then he began to backtrack laboriously along the cord, searching for an alternate power source. He would jerrybuild a tap and go on. He had no choice. It was his life. His movements were jerky, painfully slow, a metal man in search of an oilcan. He would have to splice in an extra-long, heavy-duty extension that would not fail him again. But time ran out; time stopped, and it was too late for anything: too late for help, for divine intervention or for surcease of any kind, ever.

Martin snapped the television off and sat staring as the image disappeared in a thick, murky cloud of color.

5/ It Will Be Here Soon

"It will be here soon," said the mother.

"What will?"

"The moving truck, what else? Won't that be nice?"

Martin sat at the table, picking at his breakfast. With his left hand he leafed through the class reunion program. Through the window, he saw the gaunt figure of his father; he had finished his morning walk and was now fooling with some of the cartons from the garage. A few boxes were still inside, next to the kitchen door; these, Martin knew, would be the last to go. The tools of his research.

The mother finished wrapping the last of her dishes in newspaper. She had grown cheerfully plump, he noticed, and, perhaps for the first time since his dad had married her, she was humming to herself under her breath. "He talked to you last night," she said.

"Yes."

He went on thumbing through the book. He came upon a page listing several people he thought he had known once. Each had been allotted a paragraph summary of the last fifteen years. He recognized the name of a boy who had been his best friend.

"I knew it," she said. She wiped her hands and turned around in the kitchen, distracted, as if trying to spot some small betraying detail. He knew she wanted his plate. He didn't move. "Well, he surely won't need any of that nonsense to keep him occupied once we're settled into Greenworth. A man of his age ..."

She knew his eyes were on her and stopped.

"I'll just see to the rosebushes," she said. "The new people made me promise to leave them, but I've packed away enough cuttings."

He didn't watch her leave.

He returned to the book. There was the name of his best friend. "... *Bill and Cathleen enjoy water sports, horseback riding, camping and life. The proud parents of Kevin and Teri Lynn, they presently reside in Santa Mara, where Bill is*

General Manager of the Lee Bros. Shoe Mart ..."

He stood up.

He saw his father at the curb, waiting like an animal for the exterminator. Slowly Martin walked to the door. His hand touched a box.

The deck had been re-packed in the original shipping container. He ran his fingers over the brushed aluminum and molded plastic. The tapes were arranged around the edges of the box like eggs in a carton.

He wandered back to the kitchen table. He turned another page, started to skim the book, then snatched it up and pitched it into the trash can.

He looked out again at his father, who was now ambling out of sight around the garage, head down, as if watching for cracks in the cement.

Martin picked up a carton. He would carry it outside, wait for the moving truck and put it in himself so that nothing would be broken. He could do that much. And the box underneath. It was probably full of more tapes. He flipped it open with his shoe.

He saw a large, misshapen white object.

He set the box down. The object looked like plaster of Paris. He touched it. It was a cast, bent and molded to fit an arm and part of a shoulder, the cast his father had been fitted for at the hospital, after the fall. The whitewash was smudged, dirty and — he bent closer.

It was covered with graffiti. Probably the signatures of nurses, patients. But in among the angular, unreadable letters were the words *Do you know the way to Santa Mara?*

What the hell? he wondered. Was this the message "they" had left behind? He read it again.

It was, unmistakably, his father's handwriting.

He sighed, shaking his head. He pictured the old man saving the cast after it was removed, hiding it, perhaps even dragging it out every evening and sitting there in front of his TV or his machinery, lost between his earphones, waiting for a sign that they had come again. Like the Cargo Cult out in the South Pacific. Waiting, with the sign he believed he had been given, that had come from the inscape of a fever dream. Waiting. For the return of the gods and their answers and their salvation. It wasn't true, of course. It never was. But, he thought, maybe, just maybe there is a key to some kind of truth in the asking, in the very questioning itself; maybe; maybe there is, after all.

I want to be out there, he thought, to be there with him, next to him.

But before he went outside, he knelt down and gingerly removed the deck, disturbing the arrangement of tapes as little as possible. He set it on the linoleum, unwound the cord and plugged it into the wall. He found the mike, the headphones and the last tape his father had recorded, the one not yet covered with check marks, the one that had yet to be monitored.

He inserted it, connected the microphone and headset and started the cassette. He listened to the rushing of blank tape for several minutes. Once he seemed to hear a real sound, only to recognize it as the faint crying of the pups down the block, a plaintive weeping that had been picked up during his father's recording. Then, with perfect precision, with perhaps the greatest care he had ever taken in his life, with one eye on the window and one eye on the mechanism, he depressed the SOUND-ON-SOUND RECORD button, uncovered the microphone, lifted it to his lips and, in the weakest and most unrecognizable voice he could muster, began to whisper calculatedly inarticulate, mysterious and indecipherable syllables onto the track.

Dennis Etchison

DEATHTRACKS

ANNOUNCER: Hey, let's go into this apartment and help this housewife take a shower!

ASSISTANT: Rad!

ANNOUNCER: Excuse me, ma'am!

HOUSEWIFE: Eeek!

ANNOUNCER: It's okay, I'm the New Season Man!

HOUSEWIFE: You — you came right through my TV!

ANNOUNCER: That's because there's no stopping good news! Have
you heard about New Season Body Creamer? It's guaranteed better than your old-fashioned soap product, cleaner
than water on the air! It's —

ASSISTANT: Really rad!

HOUSEWIFE: Why, you're so right! Look at the way New Season's
foaming away my dead, unwanted dermal cells! My world
has a whole new complexion! My figure has a glossy new
paisley shine! The kind that men ...

ANNOUNCER: And women!

HOUSEWIFE: ... love to touch!

ANNOUNCER: Plus the kids'll love it, too!

HOUSEWIFE: You bet they will! Wait till my husband gets up!
Why, I'm going to spend the day spreading the good news
all over our entire extended family! It's—

ANNOUNCER: It's a whole New Season!

HOUSEWIFE: A whole new reason! It's —

ASSISTANT: Absolutely RAD-I-CAL!

The young man fingered the edges of the pages with great care, almost as if they were razor blades. Then he removed his fingertips from the clipboard and tapped them along the luminous crease in his pants, one, two, three, four, five, four, three, two, one, stages of flexion about to become a silent drum-roll of boredom. With his other hand he checked his watch, clicked his pen and smoothed the top sheet of the questionnaire, circling the paper in a cursive, impatient holding pattern.

Across the room another man thumbed a remote-control device until the TV voices became silvery whispers, like ants crawling over aluminum foil.

"Walt, Bob." On the other side of the darkening living room a woman stirred in her beanbag chair, her hair shining under the black light. "It's time for *The Fuzzy Family*."

The man, her husband, shifted his buttocks in his own beanbag chair and yawned. The chair's styrofoam filling crunched like cornflakes under his weight. "Saw this one before," he said. "Besides, there's no laughtrack. They use three cameras and a live audience, remember?"

"But it might be, you know, boosted," said the woman. "Oh, what do they call it?"

"Technically augmented?" offered the young man.

They both looked at him, as though they had forgotten he was in their home.

The young man forced an unnatural, professional smile. In the black light his teeth shone too brightly.

"Right," said the man. "Not *The Fuzzy Family*, though. I filtered out a track last night. It's all new. I'm sure."

The young man was confused. He had the inescapable feeling that they were skipping (or was it simply that he was missing?) every third or fourth sentence. *I'm sure.* Sure of what? That this particular TV show had been taped

192

before an all-live audience? How could he be sure? And why would anyone care enough about such a minor technical point to bother to find out? Such things weren't supposed to matter to the blissed-out masses. Certainly not to AmiDex survey families. Unless ...

Could he be that lucky?

The questionnaire might not take very long, after all.

This one, he thought, has got to work in the industry.

He checked the computer stats at the top of the questionnaire: MORRISON, ROBERT, AGE 54, UNEMPLOYED. Used to work in the industry, then. A TV cameraman, a technician of some kind, maybe for a local station? There had been so many layoffs in the last few months, with QUBE and Teletext and all the new cable licenses wearing away at the traditional network share. And any connection, past or present, would automatically disqualify this household. Hope sprang up in his breast like an accidental porno broadcast in the middle of *Sermonette.*

He flicked his pen rapidly between cramped fingers and glanced up, eager to be out of here and home to his own video cassettes. Not to mention, say, a Bob's Big Boy hamburger, heavy relish, hold the onions and add avocado, to be picked up on the way?

"I've been sent here to ask you about last month's Viewing Log," he began. "When one doesn't come back in the mail, we do a routine follow-up. It may have been lost by the post office. I see here that your phone's been disconnected. Is that right?"

He waited while the man used the remote selector. Onscreen, silent excerpts of this hour's programming blipped by channel by channel: reruns of *Cop City,* the syndicated version of *The Cackle Factory,* the mindless *Make Me Happy, The World as We Know It, T.H.U.G.S.,* even a repeat of that PBS documentary on Teddy Roosevelt, *A Man, a Plan, a Canal, Panama,* and the umpteenth replay of *Mork and Mindy,* this the infamous last episode that had got the series canceled, wherein Mindy is convinced she's carrying Mork's alien child and nearly OD's on a homeopathic remedy of Humphrey's Eleven Tablets and blackstrap molasses. Still he waited.

"There really isn't much I need to know." He put on a friendly, stupid, shit-eating grin, hoping it would show in the purple light and then afraid that it would. "What you watch is your own business, naturally. AmiDex isn't interested in influencing your viewing habits. If we did, I guess that would undermine the statistical integrity of our sample, wouldn't it?"

Morrison and his wife continued to stare into their flickering 12-inch Sony portable.

If they're so into it, I wonder why they don't have a bigger set, one of those new picture-frame projection units from Mad Man Muntz, for example? I don't even see a Betamax. What was Morrison talking about when he said he'd taped *The Fuzzy Family?* The man had said that, hadn't he?

It was becoming difficult to concentrate.

Probably it was the black light, that and the old Day-Glow posters, the random clicking of the beaded curtains. Where did they get it all? Sitting in their living room was like being in a time machine, a playback of some Hollywood Sam Katzman or Albert Zugsmith version of the sixties; he almost expected Jack Nicholson or Luanna Anders to show up. Except that the artifacts seemed to be genuine, and in mint condition. There were things he had never seen before, not even in catalogues. His parents would know. It all must have been saved out of some weird pre-science, in anticipation of the current run on psychedelic nostalgia. It would cost a fortune to find practically *any* original black-light posters, however primitive. The one in the corner, for instance, "Ship of Peace," mounted next to "Ass Id" and an original Crumb "Keep on Truckin'" from the Print Mint in San Francisco, had been offered on the KCET auction just last week for $450, he remembered.

He tried again.

"Do you have your Viewing Log handy?" Expectantly he paused a beat. "Or did you — misplace it?"

"It won't tell you anything," said the man.

"We watch a lot of oldies," said the woman.

The young man pinched his eyes shut for a moment to clear his head. "I know what you mean," he said, hoping to put them at ease. "I can't get enough of *The Honeymooners,* myself. That Norton." He added a conspiratorial chuckle. "Sometimes I think they get better with age. They don't make 'em like that anymore. But, you know, the local affiliates would be very interested to know that you're watching."

"Not that old," said the woman. "We like the ones from the sixties. And some of the new shows, too, if —"

Morrison inclined his head toward her, so that the young man could not see, and mouthed what may have been a warning to his wife.

Suddenly and for reasons he could not name, the young man felt that he ought to be out of here.

He shook his wrist, pretending that his collector's item Nixon-Agnew watch was stuck. "What time is it getting to be?" Incredibly, he noticed that his watch had indeed stopped. Or had he merely lost track of the time? The hands read a quarter to six. Where had they been the last time he looked? "I really should finish up and get going. You're my last interview of the day. You folks must be about ready for dinner."

"Not so soon," said the woman. "It's almost time for *The Uncle Jerry Show.*"

That's a surprise, he thought. It's only been on for one season.

"Ah, that's a new show, isn't it?" he said, again feeling that he had missed something. "It's only been on for —"

Abruptly the man got up from his beanbag chair and crossed the room.

He opened a cabinet, revealing a stack of shipment cartons from the Columbia Record Club. The young man made out the titles of a few loose albums, "greatest hits" collections from groups which, he imagined, had long since disbanded. Wedged into the cabinet, next to the records, was a state-of-the-art audio frequency equalizer with graduated slide controls covering several octaves. This was patched into a small black accessory amplifier box, the

The Dark Country   **195**

kind that are sold for the purpose of connecting a TV set to an existing home stereo system. Morrison leaned over and punched a sequence of preset buttons, and without further warning a great hissing filled the room.

"This way we don't miss anything," said the wife.

The young man looked around. Two enormous Voice-of-the-Theatre speakers, so large they seemed part of the walls, had sputtered to life on either side of the narrow room. But as yet there was no sound other than the unfathomable, rolling hiss of spurious signal-to-noise output, the kind of distortion he had heard once when he set his FM receiver between stations and turned the volume up all the way.

Once the program began, he knew, the sound would be deafening.

"So," he said hurriedly, "why don't we wrap this up, so I can leave you two to enjoy your evening? All I need are the answers to a couple of quick questions, and I'll be on my way."

Morrison slumped back into place, expelling a rush of air from his beanbag chair, and thumbed the remote channel selector to a blank station. A pointillist pattern of salt-and-pepper interference swarmed the 12-inch screen. He pushed up the volume in anticipation, so as not to miss a word of *The Uncle Jerry Show* when the time came to switch channels again, eyed a clock on the wall over the Sony — there was a clock, after all, if only one knew where to look amid the glowing clutter—and half-turned to his visitor. The clock read ten minutes to six.

"What are *you* waiting to hear?" asked Morrison.

"Yes," said his wife, "why don't you tell us?"

The young man lowered his eyes to his clipboard, seeking the briefest possible explanation, but saw only the luminescence of white shag carpeting through his transparent vinyl chair — another collector's item. He felt uneasy circulation twitching his weary legs, and could not help but notice the way the inflated chair seemed to be throbbing with each pulse.

"Well," trying one more time, noting that it was com-

196

ing up on nine minutes to six and still counting, "your names were picked by AmiDex demographics. Purely at random. You represent twelve thousand other viewers in this area. What you watch at any given hour determines the rating points for each network."

There, that was simple enough, wasn't it? No need to go into the per-minute price of sponsor ad time buys based on the overnight share, sweeps week, the competing services each selling its own brand of accuracy. Eight-and-a-half minutes to go.

"The system isn't perfect, but it's the best way we have so far of —"

"You want to know why we watch what we watch, don't you?"

"Oh no, of course not! That's really no business of ours. We don't care. But we do need to tabulate viewing records, and when yours wasn't returned —"

"Let's talk to him," said the woman. "He might be able to help."

"He's too young, can't you see that, Jenny?"

"I beg your pardon?" said the young man.

"It's been such a long time," said the woman, rising with a whoosh from her chair and stepping in front of her husband. "We can try."

The man got slowly to his feet, his arms and torso long and phosphorescent in the peculiar mix of ultraviolet and television light. He towered there, considering. Then he took a step closer.

The young man was aware of his own clothing unsticking from the inflated vinyl, crackling slightly, a quick seam of blue static shimmering away across the back of the chair; of the snow pattern churning on the untuned screen, the color tube shifting hues under the black light, turning to gray, then brightening in the darkness, locking on an electric blue, and holding.

Morrison seemed to undergo a subtle transformation as details previously masked by shadow now came into focus. It was more than his voice, his words. It was the full size of him, no longer young but still strong, on his feet and braced in an unexpectedly powerful stance. It was the configuration of his head in silhouette, the haunted pallor of the skin, stretched taut, the large, luminous whites of the eyes, burning like radium. It was all these things and more. It was the reality of him, no longer a statistic but a man, clear and unavoidable at last.

The young man faced Morrison and his wife. The palms of his hands were sweating coldly. He put aside the questionnaire.

Six minutes to six.

"I'll put down that you — you declined to participate. How's that? No questions asked."

He made ready to leave.

"It's been such a long time," said Mrs. Morrison again.

Mr. Morrison laughed shortly, a descending scale ending in a bitter, metallic echo that cut through the hissing. "I'll bet it's all crazy to you, isn't it? This stuff."

"No, not at all. Some of these pieces are priceless. I recognized that right away."

"Are they?"

"Sure," said the young man. "If you don't mind my saying so, it reminds me of my brother Jack's room. He threw out most of his underground newspapers, posters, that sort of thing when he got drafted. It was back in the sixties — I can barely remember it. If only he'd realized. Nobody saved anything. That's why it's all so valuable now."

"We did," said Mrs. Morrison.

"So I see."

They seemed to want to talk, after all — lonely, perhaps — so he found himself ignoring the static and actually making an effort to prolong his exit. A couple of minutes more wouldn't hurt. They're not so bad, the Morrisons, he thought. I can see that now.

"Well, I envy you. I went through a Marvel Comics phase when I was a kid. Those are worth a bundle now, too. My mother burned them all when I went away to college, of course. It's the same principle. But if I could go back in a time machine ..." He shook his head and allowed an unforced smile to show through.

"These were our son's things," said Mrs. Morrison.

"Oh?" Could be I remind them of their son. I guess I should be honored.

"Our son David," said Mr. Morrison.

"I see." There was an awkward pause. The young man felt vaguely embarrassed. "It's nice of him to let you hold his collection. You've got quite an investment here."

The minute hand of the clock on the wall ground through its cycle, pressing forward in the rush of white noise from the speakers.

"David Morrison." Her voice sounded hopeful. "You've heard the name?"

David Morrison, David Morrison. Curious. Yes, he could almost remember something, a magazine cover or ...

"It was a long time ago. He — our son — was the last American boy to be killed in Vietnam."

It was four minutes to six and he didn't know what to say.

"When it happened, we didn't know what to think," said Mrs. Morrison. "We talked to people like us. Mostly they wanted to pretend it never happened."

"They didn't understand, either," said Mr. Morrison.

"So we read everything. The magazines, books. We listened to the news commentators. It was terribly confusing. We finally decided even they didn't know any more than we did about what went on over there, or why."

"What was it to them? Another story for *The Six O'Clock News,* right, Jenny?"

Mrs. Morrison drew a deep, pained breath. Her eyes fluttered as she spoke, the television screen at her back lost in a grainy storm of deep blue snow.

"Finally the day came for me to clear David's room ..."

"Please," said the young man, "you don't have to explain."

But she went ahead with it, a story she had gone over so many times she might have been recalling another life. Her eyes opened. They were dry and startlingly clear.

It was three minutes to six.

The Dark Country   **199**

"I started packing David's belongings. Then it occurred to us that *he* might have known the reason. So we went through his papers and so forth, even his record albums, searching. So much of it seemed strange, in another language, practically from another planet. But we trusted that the answer would be revealed to us in time."

"We're still living with it," said Morrison. "It's with us when we get up in the morning, when we give up at night. Sometimes I think I see a clue there, the way *he* would have seen it, but then I lose the thread and we're back where we started.

"We tried watching the old reruns, hoping they had something to tell. But they were empty. It was like nothing important was going on in this country back then."

"Tell him about the tracks, Bob."

"I'm getting to it ... Anyway, we waited. I let my job go, and we were living off our savings. It wasn't much. It's almost used up by now. But we had to have the answer. Why? Nothing was worth a damn, otherwise ...

"Then, a few months ago, there was this article in *TV GUIDE*. About the television programs, the way they make them. They take the tracks — the audience reactions, follow? — and use them over and over. Did you know that?"

"I — I had heard ..."

"Well, it's true. They take pieces of old soundtracks, mix them in, a big laugh here, some talk there — it's all taped inside a machine, an audience machine. The tapes go all the way back. I've broken 'em down and compared. Half the time you can hear the same folks laughing from twenty, twenty-five years ago. *And from the sixties.* That's the part that got to me. So I rigged a way to filter out everything — dialogue, music — except for the audience, the track."

"Why, he probably knows all about that. Don't you, young man?"

"A lot of them, the audience, are gone now. It doesn't matter. They're on tape. It's recycled, 'canned' they call it. It's all the same to TV. Point is, this is the only way left for us to get through, or them to us. To make contact. To listen, eavesdrop, you might say, on what folks were doing and thinking and commenting on and laughing over back then.

"I can't call 'em up on the phone, or take a poll, or stop people on the street, 'cause they'd only act like nothing happened. Today, it's all passed on. Don't ask me how, but it has.

"They're passed on now, too, so many of 'em."

"Like the boys," said Mrs. Morrison softly, so that her voice was all but lost in the hiss of the swirling blue vortex. "So many beautiful boys, the ones who would talk now, if only they could."

"Like the ones on the tracks," said Mr. Morrison.

"Like the ones who never came home," said his wife. *Dead now, all dead and never coming back.*"

One minute to six.

"Not yet," he said aloud, frightened by his own voice.

As Mr. Morrison cranked up the gain and turned back to his set, the young man hurried out. As Mrs. Morrison opened her ears and closed her eyes to all but the laugh-track that rang out around her, he tried in vain to think of a way to reduce it all to a few simple marks in a now point-less language on sheets of printed paper. And as the Morrisons listened for the approving bursts of laughter and murmuring and applause, separated out of an otherwise meaningless echo from the past, he closed the door behind him, leaving them as he had found them. He began to walk fast, faster, and finally to run.

The questionnaire crumpled and dropped from his hand.

Jack, I loved you, did you know that? You were my brother. I didn't understand, either. No one did. There was no time. But I told you, didn't I? Didn't I?

He passed other isolated houses on the block, ghostly living rooms turning to flickering beacons of cobalt blue against the night. The voices from within were television voices, muffled and anonymous and impossible to deci-pher unless one were to listen too closely, more closely than life itself would seem to want to permit, to the exclu-sion of all else, as to the falling of a single blade of grass or the unseen whisper of an approaching scythe. And it rang out around him then, too, through the trees and into the sky and the cold stars, the sound of the muttering and the laughter, the restless chorus of the dead, spreading rapidly away from him across the city and the world.

THE DARK COUNTRY

Martin sat by the pool, the wind drying his hair.

A fleshy, airborne spider appeared on the edge of the book which he had been reading there. From this angle it cast a long, pointed needle across the yellowing page. The sun was hot and clean; it went straight for his nose. Overweight American children practiced their volleyball on the bird-of-paradise plants. Weathered rattan furniture gathered dust beyond the peeling diving board.

Traffic passed on the road. Trucks, campers, bikes.

The pool that would not be scraped till summer. The wooden chairs that had been ordered up from the States. Banana leaves. Olive trees. A tennis court that might be done next year. A single color TV antenna above the palms. By the slanted cement patio heliotrope daisies, speckled climbing vines. The morning a net of light on the water. Boats fishing in Todos Santos Bay.

A smell like shrimps Veracruz blowing off the silvered waves.

And a strangely familiar island, like a hazy floating giant, where the humpback whales play. Yesterday in Ensenada, the car horns talking and a crab taco in his hand, he had wanted to buy a pair of huaraches and a Mexican shirt. The best tequila in the world for three-and-a-half a liter. Noche Buena beer, foil labels that always peel before you can read them. Delicados con Filtros cigarettes.

Bottles of agua mineral. Tehuacan con gas. *No retornable.*

He smiled as he thought of churros at the Blow Hole, the maid who even washed his dishes, the Tivoli Night Club with Reno cocktail napkins, mescal flavored with worm, eggs fresh from the nest, chorizo grease in the pan, bar girls with rhinestone-studded Aztec headbands, psychoactive liqueurs, seagulls like the tops of valentines, grilled corvina with lemon, the endless plumes of surf ...

It was time for a beer run to the bottling factory in town.

"¡Buenos diás!"

Martin looked up, startled. He was blinded by the light. He fumbled his dark glasses down and moved his head. A man and a woman stood over his chair. The sun was at their backs.

"¿Americano?"

"Yes," said Martin. He shielded his forehead and tried to see their faces. Their features were blacked in by the glare that spilled around their heads.

"I told you he was an American," said the woman. "Are you studying?"

"What?"

Martin closed the book self-consciously. It was a paperback edition of *The Penal Colony,* the only book he had been able to borrow from any of the neighboring cabins. Possibly it was the only book in Quintas Papagayo. For some reason the thought depressed him profoundly, but he had brought it poolside anyway. It seemed the right thing to do. He could not escape the feeling that he ought to be doing something more than nursing a tan. And the magazines from town were all in Spanish.

He slipped his sketchbook on top of Kafka and opened it awkwardly.

"I'm supposed to be working," he said. "On my drawings. You know how it is." They didn't, probably, but he went on. "It's difficult to get anything done down here."

"He's an artist!" said the woman.

"My wife thought you were an American student on vacation," said the man.

"Our son is a student, you see," said the woman. Martin didn't, but nodded sympathetically. She stepped aside to sit on the arm of another deck chair under the corrugated green fiberglass siding. She was wearing a sleeveless blouse and thigh-length shorts. "He was studying for his Master's Degree in Political Science at UCLA, but now he's decided not to finish. I tried to tell him he should at least get his teaching credential, but —"

"Our name's Winslow," said the man, extending a muscular hand. "Mr. and Mrs. Winslow."

"Jack Martin."

"It was the books," said Mr. Winslow. "Our boy always has books with him, even on visits." He chuckled and shook his head.

Martin nodded.

"You should see his apartment," said Mrs. Winslow. "So many." She gestured with her hands as if describing the symptoms of a hopeless affliction.

There was an embarrasing lull. Martin looked to his feet. He flexed his toes. The right ones were stiff. For something further to do, he uncapped a Pilot Fineliner pen and touched it idly to the paper. Without realizing it, he smiled. This trip must be doing me more good than I'd hoped, he thought. I haven't been near a college classroom in fifteen years.

A wave rushed toward the rocks at the other side of the cabins.

"Staying long?" asked the man, glancing around nervously. He was wearing Bermuda shorts over legs so white they were almost phosphorescent.

"I'm not sure," said Martin.

"May I take a peek at your artwork?" asked the woman.

He shrugged and smiled.

She lifted the sketchbook from his lap with infinite delicacy, as the man began talking again.

He explained that they owned their own motor home, which was now parked on the Point, at the end of the rock beach, above the breakwater. Weekend auto insurance cost them $13.70 in Tijuana. They came down whenever they got the chance. They were both retired, but there were other things to consider — just what, he did not say. But it was not the same as it used to be. He frowned at the moss growing in the bottom of the pool, at the baby weeds poking up through the sand in the canister ash trays, at the separating layers of the sawed-off diving board.

Martin could see more questions about to surface behind the man's tired eyes. He cleared his throat and squirmed in his chair, feeling the sweat from his arms soaking into the unsealed wood. Mr. Winslow was right, of course. Things were not now as they once were. But he did not relish being reminded of it, not now, not here.

A small figure in white darted into his field of vision, near the edge of the first cabin. It was walking quickly, perhaps in this direction.

"There's my maid," he said, leaning forward. "She must be finished now." He unstuck his legs from the chaise longue.

"She has keys?" said the man.

"I suppose so. Yes, I'm sure she does. Well —"

"Does she always remember to lock up?"

He studied the man's face, but a lifetime of apprehensions were recorded there, too many for Martin to isolate one and read it accurately.

"I'll remind her," he said, rising.

He picked up his shirt, took a step toward Mrs. Winslow and stood shifting his weight.

Out of the corner of his eye, he saw the maid put a hand to the side of her face.

Mrs. Winslow closed the pad, smoothed the cover and handed it back. "Thank you," she said oddly.

Martin took it and offered his hand. He realized at once that his skin had become uncomfortably moist, but Mr. Winslow gripped it firmly and held it. He confronted Martin soberly, as if about to impart a bit of fatherly advice.

"They say he comes down out of the hills," said Winslow, his eyes unblinking. Martin half-turned to the low, tan range that lay beyond the other side of the highway. When he turned back, the man's eyes were waiting. "He's been doing it for years. It's something of a legend around here. They can't seem to catch him. We never took it seriously, until now."

"Is that right?"

"Why, last night, while we were asleep, he stole an envelope of traveler's checks and a whole carton of cigarettes from behind our heads. Can you beat that? Right inside the camper! Of course we never bothered to lock up. Why should we? Everyone's very decent around here. We've never had any trouble ourselves. Until this trip. It's hard to believe."

"Yes, it is." Martin attempted to pull back as a tingling began in his stomach. But the man continued to pump his hand, almost desperately, Martin thought.

"The best advice I can give you, young man, is to lock your doors at night. From now on. You never know."

"Thanks, I will."

"He comes out after the sun goes down." He would not let go of Martin's hand. "I figure he must hit the beach three-four in the morning, when all the lights are out. Slips right in. No one notices. And then it's too late."

Martin pretended to struggle with the books so that he could drop his hand. "Well, I hope you're able to enjoy the rest of your vacation." He eyed the maid. "Now I'd better —"

"We're warning everybody along the beach," said Winslow.

"Maybe you should report it."

"That don't do no good. They listen to your story, but there's nothing they can do."

"Good luck to you, then," said Martin.

"Thank you again," said the woman peculiarly. "And don't forget. You lock your door tonight!"

"I will," said Martin, hurrying away. I won't, that is. Will, won't, what did it matter? He sidestepped the dazzling flowers of an ice plant and ascended the cracked steps of the pool enclosure. He crossed the paved drive and slowed.

The maid had passed the last of the beachfront houses and was about to intersect his path. He waited for her to greet him as she always did. I should at least pretend to talk to her, he thought, in case the Winslows are still watching. He felt their eyes, or someone's, close at his back.

"*Buenos diás,*" he said cheerfully.

She did not return the greeting. She did not look up. She wagged her head and trotted past, clutching her uniform at the neck.

He paused and stared after her. He wondered in passing about her downcast eyes, and about the silent doorways of the other cabins, though it was already past ten o'clock. And then he noticed the scent of ozone that now laced the air, though no thunderhead was visible yet on the horizon, only a gathering fog far down the coastline, wisps of it beginning to striate the wide, pale sky above the sagging telephone poles. And he wondered about the unsteadiness in Mrs. Winslow's voice as she had handed back the sketchbook. It was not until he was back at the beach that he remembered: the pages he had shown her were blank. There were no sketches at all yet in the pad, only the tiny flowing blot he had made with his pen on the first sheet while they talked, like a miniature misshapen head or something else, something else, stark and unreadable on the crisp white sulfite paper.

He was relieved to see that the private beach had finally come alive with its usual quota of sunbathers. Many of them had probably arisen early, shortly after he'd left for the quiet of the pool, and immediately swarmed to the surf with no thought of TV or the morning paper, habits they had left checked at the border sixty miles from here. A scattered few lagged back, propped out on their patios, sipping coffee and keeping an eye on the children who were bounding through the spume. The cries of the children and of the gulls cut sharply through the waves which, disappointingly, were beginning to sound to Martin like nothing so much as an enormous screenful of ball bearings.

There was the retired rent-a-cop on holiday with his girlfriend, stretched out on a towel and intent on his leg exercises. There was the middle-aged divorcée from two doors down, bent over the tidepools, hunting for moon-stones among jealous clusters of aquamarine anemones. And there was Will, making time with the blonde in the blue tank top. He seemed to be explaining to her some sort of diagram in the slicked sand between the polished stones. Martin toed into his worn rubber sandals and went down to join them.

"Want to go to a party?" Will said to him as he came up.

"When?"

"Whenever," said the blonde in the blue top. She tried to locate Martin's face, gave up and gazed back in the general direction of the southern bungalows.

There a party was still in progress, as it had been since last Wednesday, when Will and Martin had arrived. The other party, the one on the north side, had apparently been suspended for a few hours, though just now as Martin watched a penny rocket streaked into the sky from the bathroom window, leaving an almost invisible trail of pow-der-blue smoke in the air above the water. The skyrocket exploded with a faint report like a distant rifle and began spiraling back to earth. Martin heard hoarse laughter and the sudden cranking-up of stereo speakers inside the slid-ing doors. So the party there was also nearly in full swing again, or had never let up. Perhaps it was all one big party, with his cabin sandwiched like a Christian Science reading room between two pirate radio stations. He remembered the occasional half-dressed teenager staggering around the firepit and across his porch last night, grunting about more beer and did he know where those nurses were staying? Martin had sat outside till he fell asleep, seeing them piss their kidneys out on the steaming stones by the footpath.

"Bummer," said the girl seriously. Martin noticed that she was lugging around an empty twelve-ounce bottle. She upended it and a few slippery drops hit the rocks. "You guys wouldn't know where the Dos Equis's stashed, would-jou?"

"*No es problema,* my dear," said Will, steering her toward the patio.

Martin followed. Halfway there the girl wobbled around and hurled the bottle as high as she could away from the shoreline. Unfortunately, her aim was not very good. Martin had to duck. He heard it whistle end-over-end over his head and shatter on the flat rocks. Will caught her under the arms and staggered her inside. Next door, a Paul Simon song was playing on the tape deck.

By the time Martin got there she was on her way out, cradling a bottle of Bohemia. Again she tried to find his eyes, gave up and began picking her way across the rocks.

"Take it slow," yelled Will. "Hey, sure you don't want to lie down for a while?"

Martin grinned at him and walked past into the high-beamed living room. The fireplace was not lighted, nor was the wall heater, but a faint but unmistakable odor of gas lingered in the corners.

"We better stock up on Dos Equis from now on," said Will.

"Is that her favorite?"

"She doesn't care. But we shelled out a deposit on the case of Bohemia. Dos Equis is no return."

Martin stood staring out at the island in the bay. The fishing boats were moving closer to shore. Now he could barely make out the details of the nearest one. He squinted. It wasn't a fishing boat at all, he realized. It was much larger than he had imagined, some kind of oil tanker, perhaps. "Guess what, Will? We're going to have to start locking the doors."

"Why? Afraid the *putas* are gonna OD on Spanish fly and jump our bones in the middle of the night?"

"You wish," said Martin. He sniffed around the heater, then followed the scent to the kitchen and the stove. "The gas pilots," he said. "It's the draft. You — we're — always going in and out. The big door's open all the time."

"Got a match, man?" Will took out a bent cigarette, straightened it and crumpled the pack. The table was littered with empty packs of cheap Mexican cigarettes, Negritos and Faros mostly. Martin wondered how his friend could smoke such garbage. He took out his Zippo. Will struck it with an exaggerated shaking of his hands, but it was out of fluid. He stooped over the gas stove and winked at Martin. He turned the knob. The burner lit. He inhaled, coughed and reached for the tequila. He poured himself a tall one mixed with grapefruit juice. "Mmm. Good for the throat, but it still burns a little."

"Your system runs on alcohol, Willy. You know that, don't you?"

"Don't all machines?"

"Myself, I could go for some eggs right now. How about you? What've we got left?" Martin went to the sink. It was full of floating dishes. "Hey, what the hell is it with the maid? We did remember to leave her a tip yesterday. Didn't we?"

"One of us must have."

That was it, then. That was why she had skipped them, and then snubbed him this morning. That had to be it. Didn't it?

The tape deck next door was now blaring a golden oldie by Steely Dan. Martin slid the glass door closed. Then he snagged his trousers from the back of a chair and put them on over his trunks. Started to put them on. They did not feel right. He patted his back pocket.

Will slid the door back open halfway. "You're serious, aren't you? Look at it this way. Leave it like this and the gas'll just blow on outside. Relax, man. That's what you came down here for, isn't it? After what happened, you need ..."

Martin checked the chair. On the table were a deck of playing cards from a Mission Bay savings and loan, the backs of which were imprinted with instructions about conserving energy, a Mexican wrestling magazine with a cover picture of the masked hero, El Santo, in the ring against a hooded character in red jumpsuit and horns, and an old mineral water bottle full of cigarette butts. On the floor, lying deflated between the table legs, was his wallet.

"There's another reason, I'm afraid." Martin twisted open the empty wallet and showed it to his friend.

"Who in the hell ...?"

"Well, it certainly wasn't the maid. Look at this place." Outside, a small local boy came trudging through the patios. He was carrying a leather case half as big as he was. He hesitated at the cabin on the south side, as three teen-aged American boys, their hair layered identically and parted in the middle, called their girls out into the sun. "It must have happened during the night."

"Christ!" said Will. He slapped the tabletop. He reached for his own wallet. It was intact. "There. I was over there partying all night, remember? They must've passed by every place where anybody was still up."

The small boy opened his case and the American girls began poring excitedly over a display of Indian jewelry, rings and belt buckles and necklaces of bright tooled silver and turquoise. From a distance, an old man watched the boy and waited, nodding encouragement.

"You should have gone with me," said Will. "I told you. Well, don't you worry, Jack. I've got plenty here for both of us."

"No, man. I can wire my agent or —"

"Look," said Will, "I can even kite a check if I have to, to cover the rental till we get back. They'll go for it. I've been coming here since I was a kid."

I've got to get away from here, thought Martin. No, that isn't right. Where else is there to go? I've come this far already just to get away. It's hopeless. It always was. You can run, he told himself, but you can't hide. Why didn't I realize that?

"Here," said Will. "Here's twenty for now."

"Are you sure?"

"Don't worry about it. I'd better go see if the nurses got hit, too. Saw a bunch of people in a huddle down the beach a while ago." He drained his glass. "Then I'll make another beer run. The hell with it. We're gonna party tonight, God damn it! You going by the office, Jack?"

"Sure."

"Then you might as well report it to the old lady. I think she's got a son or a nephew in the federales. Maybe they can do something about it."

"Maybe," said Martin, cracking open a beer. He could have told Will that it wouldn't do any good. He stopped in at the office anyway. It didn't.

He wandered on up the highway to Enrique's Cafe. On the way he passed a squashed black cat, the empty skin of it in among the plants, the blood-red flowers and spotted adder's tongues and succulents by the roadside. The huevos rancheros were runny but good. When he got back, Will's four-wheel drive was still parked under the carport. He took the keys and made the beer run into town himself, police cars honking him out of the way to make left turns from right-hand lanes, zigzagging across the busy intersections of the city to avoid potholes. He bought a case of Dos Equis and, for forty cents more, a liter of soft, hot tortillas. As the afternoon wore on he found himself munching them, rolled with butter and later plain, even though he wasn't really hungry.

That evening he sat alone on a bench by the rocks, hearing but not listening to a Beatles song ("Treat Me Like You Did the Night Before"), the smoke from his Delicado wafting on the breeze, blending with wood smoke from the chimneys and rising slowly to leave a smear like the Milky Way across the Pleiades. It's time for me to leave this place, he thought. Not to run away, no, not this time; but to go back. And face the rest of it, my life, no matter how terrible things may have turned back home since I left.

Not Will, though; he should stay awhile longer if he likes. True, it was my idea; he only took the time off at my suggestion, setting it all up to make me comfortable; he knew I couldn't take any more last week, the way things were up there. He's my friend. Still, he was probably waiting for just such an excuse in order to get away himself.

So I'll call or wire the agency for a plane ticket, give them a cock-and-bull story about losing everything — the truth, in other words. It was the truth, wasn't it? I'll say the trip was part of the assignment. I had to come down here to work on some new sketches for the book, to follow a lead about headstone rubbings in, let's see, Guanajuato. Only I never made it that far. I stopped off for some local color. Charge it against my royalty statement ... I'll talk to them tomorrow. Yes, tomorrow.

Meanwhile, there's still tonight ...

But I should tell Will first.

He resumed walking. There was a fire on the breakwater by the Point. He went toward it. Will would be in one of the cabins, partying with a vengeance. Martin glanced in one window. A slide show was in progress, with shots that looked like the pockmarked surface of another planet taken from space. He pressed closer and saw that these pictures were really close-ups of the faces of newborn seals or sea lions. Not that one, he thought, and moved on.

One of the parties he came to was in the big cabin two doors north of his own. That one was being rented, he remembered, by the producer of a show in the late seventies called STARSHIP DISCO. Martin had never seen it.

An Elvis Costello tape shook the walls. A young card hustler held forth around the living room table. A warm beer was pushed into Martin's hand by a girl. He popped the beer open and raised it, feeling his body stir as he considered her. Why not? But she could be my daughter, technically, he thought, couldn't she? Then: what a disgusting point of view. Then: what am I doing to myself? Then it was too late; she was gone.

Will was not in the back rooms. The shelf in the hallway held three toppling books. Well well, he thought, there are readers down here, after all. Then he examined them — *By Love Possessed* by Cozzens, *Invitation to Tea* by Monica Lang (The People's Book Club, Chicago, 1952), *The Foundling* by Francis Cardinal Spellman. They were covered with years of dust.

He ducked into the bathroom and shut the door, seeing the mirror and razor blade lying next to the sink, the roll of randomly-perforated crepe paper toilet tissue. There was a knock on the door. He excused himself and went out, and found Will in the kitchen.

"*¡Dos cervezas,* Juan!" Will was shouting. "Whoa. I feel more like I do now than when I got here!" With some prodding, he grabbed two cold ones and followed Martin outside, rubbing his eyes.

He seemed relieved to sit down.

"So," began Martin. "What did you find out? Did anyone else get popped last night?"

"Plenty! One, the nurses. Two, the bitch from San Diego. Three, the — where is it now? Ojai. Those people. The ..." He ran out of fingers. "Let's see. Anyway, there's plenty, let me tell you."

The ships were now even nearer the shore. Martin saw their black hulls closing in over the waves.

"I was thinking," he said. "Maybe it's time to go. What would you say to that, man?"

"Nobody's running scared. That's not the way to play it. You should hear 'em talk. They'll get his ass next time, whoever he is. Believe it. The kids, they didn't get hit. But three of those other guys are rangers. Plus there's the cop. See the one in there with the hat? He says he's gonna lay a trap, cut the lights about three o'clock, everybody gets quiet, then bam! You better believe it. They're mad as hell."

"But why —"

"It's the dock strike. It happens every year when there's a layoff. The locals get hungry. They swoop down out of the hills like bats."

Just then a flaming object shot straight through the open front door and fizzled out over the water. There was a hearty "All r-r-ight!" from a shadow on the porch, and then the patio was filled with pogoing bodies and clapping hands. The night blossomed with matches and fireworks, 1000-foot skyrockets, bottle rockets and volleys of Mexican cherry bombs, as the party moved outside and chose up sides for a firecracker war. Soon Martin could no longer hear himself think. He waited it out. Will was laughing.

Martin scanned the beach beneath the screaming lights. And noticed something nearby that did not belong. It was probably a weird configuration of kelp, but ... he got up and investigated.

It was only this: a child's broken doll, wedged half-under the stones. What had he supposed it was? It had been washed in on the tide, or deliberately dismembered and its parts strewn at the waterline, he could not tell which. In the flickering explosions, its rusty eye sockets appeared to be streaked with tears.

A minute after it had begun, the firecracker war was over. They sat apart from the cheering and the breaking bottles, watching the last shot of a Roman candle sizzle below the surface of the water like a green torpedo. There was scattered applause, and then a cry went up from another party house down the beach as a new round of fireworks was launched there. Feet slapped the sand, dodging rocks.

"Do you really believe that?"

"What?"

"About someone coming down from the hills," said Martin. *Like bats.* He shuddered.

"Watch this," said Will. He took his bottle and threw it into the air, snapping it so it flew directly at a palm tree thirty feet away. It smashed into the trunk at the ragged trim line.

Instantly the treetop began to tremble. There was a high rustling and a shaking and a scurrying. And a rattling of tiny claws. A jagged frond dropped spearlike to the beach.

"See that? It's rats. The trees around here are full of 'em. You see how bushy it is on top? It never gets trimmed up there. Those rats are born, live and die in the trees. They never touch down."

"But how? I mean, what do they eat if —?"

"Dates. Those are palm trees, remember? And each other, probably. You've never seen a dead one on the ground, have you?"

Martin admitted he hadn't.

"Not that way with the bats, though. They have to come out at night. Maybe they even hit the rats. I never saw that. But they have mouths to feed, don't they? There's nothing much to eat up in the hills. It must be the same with the peasants. They have families. Wouldn't you?"

"I hate to say this. But. You did lock up, didn't you?"

216

Will laughed dryly. "Come on. I've got something for you. I think it's time you met the nurses."

Martin made a quick sidetrip to check the doors at their place, and they went on. They covered the length of the beach before Will found the porch he was looking for. Martin reached out to steady his friend, and almost fell himself. He was getting high. It was easy.

As they let themselves in, the beach glimmered at their backs with crushed abalone shells and scuttling hermit crabs. Beyond the oil tankers, the uncertain outline of the island loomed in the bay. It was called Dead Man's Island, Will told him.

He woke with the sensation that his head was cracking open. Music or something like it in the other room, throbbing through the thin walls like the pounding of surf. Voices. An argument of some kind. He brushed at the cobwebs. He had been lost in a nightmare of domination and forced acquiescence before people who meant to do him harm. It returned to him in fragments. What did it mean? He shook it off and rolled out of bed.

There was the floor he had pressed with his hand last night to stop the room from spinning. There was the nurse, tangled in the sheets next to him. He guessed she was the nurse. He couldn't see her face.

He went into the bathroom. He took a long draught of water from the faucet before he came out. He raised his head and the room spun again. The light from the window hurt his eyes — actual physical pain. He couldn't find his sock. He tottered into the other room.

A young man with blown-dry hair was playing the tape deck too loudly. The sound vibrated the bright air, which seemed thin and brittle, hammering it like beaten silver. There was the girl in the blue tank top, still seated next to the smoldering fireplace. An empty bottle of Damiana Liqueur was balanced against her thigh. Her eyes were closed and her face was stony. He wondered if she had slept that way, propped upright all night. On the table were

The Dark Country   **217**

several Parker Brothers-type games from stateside: *Gambler, Creature Features, The Game of Life.* A deck of Gaiety Brand nudie cards, with a picture on the box of a puppy pulling a bikini top out of a purse. Someone had been playing solitaire. Martin couldn't remember.

There was a commotion outside.

"What's that?" he said, shielding his eyes.

"Talking Heads," said the young man. He showed Martin the tape box. "They're pretty good. That lead guitar line is hard to play. It's so repetitious."

"No, I mean ..."

Martin scratched and went into the kitchen. It was unoccupied, except for a cricket chirping somewhere behind the refrigerator. Breakfast was in process; eggs were being scrambled in a blender the nurses had brought with them from home. Martin protected his eyes again and looked outside.

There was Will. And there were three or four tan beach boys from the other party. And the cop. He wasn't doing his leg exercises this morning. They were having an argument.

Martin stumbled out.

"But you can't do that," one of them was saying.

"Stay cool, okay, motherfuck? You want the whole beach to know?"

"You think they don't already?"

"The hell they do! We drug him over out of the way. No one'll —"

"No one but the maids!"

"That's what I'm *say*ing. You guys are a bunch of jack-offs. Jesus Christ! I'm about *this* close to kicking your ass right now, do you know that?"

"All right, all right!" said Will. "That kind of talk's just digging us in deeper. Now let's run through the facts. One —"

Martin came up. They shot looks at each other that both startled him and made him unreasonably afraid for their safety as well as his own. They stopped talking, their eyes wild, as if they had gobbled a jar of Mexican amphetamines.

Will took him aside.

"We've got to do something!" said the one with the souvenir hat. "What're you —?"

"Hold on," said Will. "We're all in this together, like it or —"

"I'm not the one who —"

"— Like it or not. Now just try to keep a tight asshole another minute, will you, while I talk to my friend Jack? It's his neck, too."

They started back up the beach. Will propelled him ahead of the others, as to a rendezvous of great urgency.

"They got him," said Will.

"Who?"

"The thief, whoever he was. Poor bastard. Two guys from next door cornered him outside our place. Sometime around dawn, the way I get it. Apparently he fell on the rocks. He's dead. They found me here a little while ago. Now —"

"What?"

"— Now there's no use shitting bricks. It's done. What we have to do is think of a way to put ourselves in the clear — fast. We're the strangers here."

"We can make it look like an accident," said the one in the hat. "Those rocks are —"

"Accident, hell," said the security cop. "It was self-defense, breaking and entering. We caught him and blew him away. No court in —"

"This isn't the USA, you dumb shit, You know what greaser jails are like? They hate our guts. All they want's our money. This buddy of mine, he got ..."

And so it went till they reached the porch, the surrounding beach littered with the casings of burnt-out rockets, vomit drying on the rocks, broken clam shells bleaching between the rocks, the rocks like skulls. And here blood, vivid beyond belief even on the bricks of the patio, great splotches and gouts of it, like gold coins burnished in the sun, a trail that led them in the unforgiving light of day to the barbecue pit and the pile of kindling stacked in the charcoal shade.

Martin knelt and tore at the logs.

And there.

The body was hidden inside a burlap sack. It was the body of the boy who had come by yesterday, the boy who had wanted to sell his jewelry.

He felt his stomach convulse. The small face was scraped raw, the long eyelashes caked and flaking, the dark skin driven from two of the ribs to show white muscle and bone. A great fear overtook Martin, like wings settling upon him, blocking out the sun. He folded under them momentarily and dry-heaved in the ashes.

Will was pacing the narrow patio like a prisoner in a cell, legs pumping out and back over the cracking cement, pivoting faster and faster at the edges until he was practically spinning, generating a hopeless rage that would not be denied but could not be released. His hands were shaking violently, and his arms and shoulders and body. He looked around with slitted eyes, chin out, lips drawn in, jaws grinding stone. Far down the beach by the Point an elderly man came walking, hesitating at each house and searching each lot. He was carrying a leather case.

Will said, "You kicked him to death, didn't you? You stomped this child until he was dead." Then, his voice a hiss, he began to curse them between his teeth with an unspeakable power and vileness. The one in the hat tried to break in. He started shouting.

"It was dark! He could've been anyone! What was he doing creepin' around here? He could've been —"

But Will was upon him, his arms corded, his fingers going for the throat. The others closed in. People on the beach were turning to stare. Martin saw it all as if in slow motion: himself rising at last to his full height, leaping into it a split-second before the others could grab hold, as he fell on their arms to stop the thumbs from Will's eyes, to break Will's hands from the other's throat. Everything stopped. Martin stepped between them as the young one fell back to the flagstone wall. Martin raised his right hand, flattened and angled it like a knife. With his left he cupped the back of the young man's neck, holding it almost tenderly. The young man's eyes were almost kind. They were eyes Martin had seen all his life, outside recruiting offices and Greyhound bus depots the years over, and they were a law unto themselves. He brought his right hand down sharp and hard across the face, again, again, three times, like pistol shots. The tan went white, then red where he had slapped it. For a moment nobody said anything. The old man kept coming.

They passed motorcycle cops, overheated VW's, Jeeps, Chevy Luvs, Ford Couriers with camper shells, off-road vehicles with heavy-duty shocks and, a mile outside of town, a half-acre of pastel gravestones by the main road. Martin fit as best he could among the plastic water jugs, sleeping bags and Instamatic cameras in the back seat. The boys from next door were piled in with him, the one in the hat in front and Will at the controls of the four-wheel drive.

The twenty-mile access road behind Ensenada wound them higher and higher, pummeling them continuously until they were certain that the tie rods or the A-frame or their bodies would shake loose and break apart at the very next turn. The lane shrank to a mere dirt strip, then to a crumbling shale-and-sandstone ledge cut impossibly around the backs of the hills, a tortuous serpentine above abandoned farmland and the unchecked acreage between the mountains and the sea. Twice at least one of the wheels left the road entirely; they had to pile out and lay wild branches under the tires to get across fissures that had no bottom. Martin felt his kidneys begin to ache under the endless pounding. One of the boys threw up and continued to retch over the side until Will decided they had gone far enough, but no one opened his mouth to complain. After more than an hour, they set the hand brake at the start of a primitive downslope, blocked the wheels with granite chips and stumbled the rest of the way, numb and reeling.

The silence was overpowering. Nothing moved, except for the random scrabbling of lizards and the falling of individual leaves and blades of grass. As they dragged the sack down to the meadows, Martin concentrated on the ribbon of dirt they had driven, watching for the first sign of another car, however unlikely that was. A small, puddled heat mirage shimmered on the dust, coiled and waiting to be splashed. A squirrel darted across the road, silhouetted as it paused in stop-motion, twitched its pointed head and then ran on, disappearing like an escaped shooting gallery target. Great powdered monarch butterflies aimlessly swam the convection currents; like back home, he thought. Yes, of course; I should have known. Only too much like home.

"Dig here," said Will.

The old wound in Martin's foot was hurting him again. He had thought it would be healed by now, but it wasn't. He rocked back wearily on one heel. A withered vine caught at his ankle. It snapped easily with a dull, fleshy sound as he shook free. He took another step, and something moist and solid broke underfoot. He looked down.

He kicked at the grass. It was only a tiny melon, one of dozens scattered nearby and dying on the vine. He rolled it over, revealing its soft underbelly. Too much rain this season, he thought absently; too much or too little, nourishing them excessively or not enough. What was the answer? He picked it up and lobbed it over their heads. It splattered on the road in a burst of pink. Watermelons, he thought, while fully-formed seeds pale as unborn larvae slithered off his shoe and into the damp grass. Who planted them here? And who will return for the harvest, only to find them already gone to seed? He stooped and wiped his hand. There was a faint but unmistakable throb and murmur in the ground, as though through a railroad track, announcing an unseen approach from miles away.

"What are you going to do, Jackie?"

Martin stared back at Will. He hadn't expected the question, not now.

"It's like this," said Will, taking him to one side. "Michael, for one, wants to get back to his own van and head on deeper into Baja, maybe San Quintin, lay low for a few days. He wasn't registered, so there's no connection. Some of the others sound like they're up for the same, or for going north right away, tonight. Kevin's due to check out today, anyway."

"And you?"

"Don't know yet. I haven't decided. I'll probably stay on for appearances, but you do what you want. I wouldn't worry about the maid or anyone coming by to check up. Anyway, we hosed off the patio. Nobody else saw a thing, I'm sure. The girls don't know anything about it." There was a grunt. The sack, being lowered, had split open at the seams. Hands hurried to reclose it.

"What's that?"

Will grabbed a wrist. A silver bracelet inlaid with polished turquoise glittered against a bronze tan in the afternoon light.

"I — I bought it."

"Sure you did," said Will.

"I brought it with me on the trip. Ask my girl. She —"

Will stripped it off the arm and flung it into the shallow grave. "You want to get out of this alive, kiddo? That kind of work can be traced. Or didn't you think of that? You didn't think, did you? What else did you steal from him while you were at it yesterday? Is that why he came back last night? Is it?"

"Lookit, man, where do you get off —"

"We all hang together," said Will, "or we all hang together. Get it?"

He got to his knees to close the sack. As an afterthought, he reached deep and rifled the dead child's pockets for anything that might tie in with Quintas Papagayo.

His hand stopped. He withdrew a wad of paper money which fell open, a flower on his palm. A roll of American dollars, traveler's checks, credit cards.

"Hey, that's —"

"I had eighty bucks on me when —"

Martin joined him in examining the roll. The checks were signed NORMAN WINSLOW. Two of the cards, embossed on the front and signed on the back, read JACK

MARTIN.

"Knew I was right!" said the one in the felt hat. "Fuck if I wasn't! Lookit that! The little son of a bitch …

Martin straight-armed the wheel, running in darkness.

He reminded himself of the five-dollar bill clipped to the back of his license. Then he remembered that his wallet was flat, except for the credit cards. Motorcycle cops passed him like fugitive Hell's Angels. He kicked on the lights of his rented car and thought of the last news tape of the great Karl Wallenda. He had been running, too, though in wind, not fog, toward or away from something.

Did he look back, I wonder? Was that why it happened?

… Heading for the end, his last that day was weak. Or maybe he looked ahead that once, saw it was the same, and just gave up the ghost. No, not Wallenda. For him the game was running while pretending not to—or the other way around. Was that his private joke? Even in Puerto Rico, for him the walk was all. *Keep your bead clear,* he wanted to tell Wallenda. For that was how it finished, stopping to consider. But Wallenda must have known; he had been walking for years. Still he should have remembered … Martin put on his brights, gripped the steering wheel and made for the border.

He turned on the radio, found an American station.

It was playing a song by a group called The Tubes. He remembered the Trivoli Night club, the elevated band playing "Around the World" and "A Kiss to Build a Dream On." He remembered Hussong's Cantina, the knife fight that happened, his trip to the Blow Hole, policia with short hair and semiautomatic rifles. The housetrailers parked on the Point, the Point obscured by mist. The military guns with silencers …

The doll whose parts had been severed, its eyes opening in moonlight.

Shaking, he turned his mind to what lay ahead. He wanted to see someone; he tried to think of her face. Her

eyes would find his there under the beam ceiling, the spider plants in the corners growing into the carpet, the waves
on Malibu beach, the Pleiades as bright, shining on what
was below: the roots between the rocks, the harbor lights
like eyes, the anemones closed inward, gourds and giant
mushrooms, the endless pull of riptide, the seagulls white
as death's-heads, the police with trimmed moustaches, the
dark ships at anchor...

He came to a bridge on the tollway. Ahead lay the border.

To his right a sign, a turnoff that would take him back
into Baja.

He sat with the motor running, trying to pick a direction.